THIS IS JUST A TEST

THIS IS JUST A TEST

A Novel by

MADELYN ROSENBERG

and

WENDY WAN-LONG SHANG

SCHOLASTIC INC.

ISBN 978-1-338-22968-4

12 11 10 9 8 7 6 5 4 3 2 1   17 18 19 20 21 22

Printed in the U.S.A.   40

First Scholastic paperback printing, October 2017

Book design by Nina Goffi

For Graham and Karina

— MR

For Matthew, Jason, and Kate

— WWS

THIS IS JUST A TEST

The closest I ever came to being a hero was when

our class took a field trip to McKimmon's Farm. It was the middle of November, and we'd already had a couple of frosts, which killed off a lot of the green things and which made us wonder whose idea it was to visit a farm this time of year. Spring would make more sense, when they were planting stuff. Or if the farm grew pumpkins, which it didn't. When we went, everything was dying on McKimmon's Farm, and that included the poison ivy, which Mr. McKimmon wasn't growing as a crop or anything; it was wild.

Wild, and, like I said, mostly dead. The sun was shining down hard on us, in that cloudless blue postcard way that happens in Virginia.

The teachers told a group of us to sit at the picnic tables so they could pass around seeds and dried gourds, which Mr. McKimmon actually did grow. Hector, my best friend, squirmed between the bench and the table and ducked underneath.

"What are you doing?" I asked. The other kids were giving Hector a look.

"It's shadier down here," Hector said. One thing I'll say about Hector is that he's not afraid to be unconventional. It used to be a quality I admired, like when Hector suggested that we do everything backward for a week, or when he signed us up for correspondence classes in French because he wanted to go to the Cannes Film Festival one day. But in junior high, unconventionality was usually another word for *dork*.

"Knock it off," I told Hector. I was pretty sure that under the transitive property of junior high social lives, whatever our group was thinking of Hector, they were going to start thinking of me. Hector popped back up.

"My little brother does that all the time," said Kelli Ann Majors. I happened to know that Kelli Ann's little brother was eight; it was one of the facts I had collected about her. It was also exactly what I was afraid someone would think.

"Watch this," said Scott Dursky, who was in a couple of my classes. Under normal circumstances, I ignored Scott and his stunts. But now he was providing a distraction—the good kind. I watched him, hoping everyone else would, too, as he walked to an oak tree that had a bunch of vines attacking the trunk. They looked like tentacles. Scott grabbed one to try to get some climbing leverage, but the vine was loose and fell out of the tree while he was holding it.

Terry Sutphin stood behind him and said, "Nice try. Let me show you how it's done." Scott grabbed a different vine for a better hold. It was furry. Even from where we were sitting, I could tell it was poison ivy.

"That's poison ivy," I told Hector. "They shouldn't be touching that."

"Hey!" Hector shouted. "That's poison ivy."

"Says who?" Scott didn't let go of the vine, though you could see his grip relax slightly.

"Says David," said Hector. We walked over to the tree.

"I don't see any leaves," said Terry.

"You can get poison ivy from the vine, too," I told him. "You know: 'Hairy vine, no friend of mine.' It still contains urushiol."

"I've never heard that," Scott said, but he let go of the vine.

"He's making it up," said Terry. He patted the vine, which looked like the tail of a scruffy cat. "This is my pet, Lucky. He would never hurt me. Don't you want to meet my pet?" He reached for the closest girl, who shrieked and ran away.

"Why would I make it up?" I said. If I were going to make something up, it would be something like: studying too much for your bar mitzvah can stunt your growth, or eating only Chinese food causes premature baldness. Personally, I would like to spend less time studying Torah and more time eating pizza.

3

"I thought the plant had to be fresh and shiny for you to catch poison ivy," said Kelli Ann, who was fresh and shiny herself. She ducked behind me to avoid Terry, who went to chase some other kids across the field.

"No," I said. "Lead deaves and vines, too." I resisted the urge to punch myself in the face. Kelli Ann had nice eyes, which made it hard for my brain to do normal things, like form words.

"Group B!" yelled Mrs. Osterberg, our science teacher. She was standing near a tractor, next to a red barn that looked as though it had been painted just for our field trip. "It's time for your hayride."

"Scott Dursky touched poison ivy," said Kelli Ann. "So did Terry Sutphin."

Mrs. Osterberg took a first aid kit out of her purse and sifted through it. There didn't seem to be much in there besides aspirin and Band-Aids. Then she looked toward the front of the farm, about a million miles away, where there was a small public bathroom. She seemed to be calculating something in her head.

"Very well," she said. "You can take the hayride with Group D. For now, go get those hands washed. With soap, Mr. Dursky. Lots and lots of soap. Mr. Horowitz? You go with him."

"But—" I said.

"Go." She turned to Hector. "Mr. Clelland, round up Mr. Sutphin and tell him to do likewise."

Kelli Ann waved as she went off on the hayride. Scott waved back, because Scott was the kind of person who always assumed that someone was waving to him. I did a low-key kind of wave, the kind that would count if she was actually waving at me, but one I could also say was for someone else if she wasn't. It would have been nice to be on the same hayride as Kelli Ann, not that I would sit directly next to her, but maybe I would sit near her and practice not feeling nervous. Instead, I had to go with Scott to the bathroom. Even though Scott and I had gone to school with each other for a couple of years, I'd never had a real conversation with him.

"If there wasn't a bathroom," I said, "you could rub lemon juice on your skin. The acid cuts through the oil."

"Where would we get lemons around here?" asked Scott. Mr. McKimmon didn't grow those, either; Virginia had the wrong climate.

"Maybe someone packed lemonade in their lunch?" I suggested. Scott seemed impressed by my idea, which gave me another one.

"And bananas," I said. "If you were too late to do anything about the oil, the inside of a banana peel will cut down on the itching."

"How does that work?"

I thought for a minute. "Maybe some kind of oil in the peel? Banana skins are also good for shining shoes." I had done a project in fourth grade on bananas. "You can even put a banana peel on your forehead to cure headaches."

"I'll bet that doesn't work," Scott said. "Though if someone standing near you had a headache, they'd probably forget about it while you were wearing your banana bandanna."

Hector found us just as Scott finished up in the bathroom. "I told Terry to come to the bathroom, and he said he wasn't interested in 'doing likewise,'" announced Hector. "Even though he had to make."

"'Make'?" repeated Scott.

Hector's mom hated what she called "bathroom" words, so Hector just said *make*, which, up to this point, had never bothered me.

"Take a leak," I translated.

"He went behind the barn," Hector said.

Scott shook his head. "That's Terry for you."

"Should we talk to him?" I asked. "Maybe he'll listen, if you tell him to wash his hands."

"He'll probably be fine," Scott said.

"*You* washed your hands," Hector pointed out.

"That's me. To me, it's a low risk/high reward situation to wash my hands."

"You really can get poison ivy from the vines," I said.

"He had his chance," said Scott. "Besides, some people don't get poison ivy."

If it hadn't been for Terry, that might have been the end of the story for Hector and me. But instead, Kelli Ann greeted us the next morning with some serious news.

"Terry Sutphin is covered in poison ivy," she said. This was my world record for talking to a girl who wasn't a family member. "Everywhere. He couldn't come to school today."

I thought about Terry taking a leak behind the barn, and shuddered. "We tried to tell him." Poison ivy would make a great weapon, but as far as I knew, the military did not engage in plant warfare. All everyone talked about these days was nuclear weapons. The thing about nukes was they were really, really powerful—there was no calamine lotion for nuclear weapons.

"He would *totally* listen to you guys now," she said.

"Maybe," I said. It was best to keep sentences short around Kelli Ann, but what I was thinking was: *Now the entire seventh grade knows about poison ivy vines.*

"I'm not sure we learned anything else useful," said Kelli Ann. "You and Hector saved the field trip. A lot more people could have gotten poison ivy if you guys hadn't said something."

I was a tiny bit irritated by the *you guys* comment, since I was the one who had noticed the vines; Hector had only been the loudspeaker. But I supposed that part was critical, too.

"You guys should get extra credit from Mrs. Osterberg," Kelli Ann said. "Scott Dursky owes you, big time."

That part, I figured, was true.

Scott found us at lunch. At first, I thought he was going to thank us for saving him. Instead, he said, "So I was thinking of entering the trivia tournament."

"Oh," I said. Because I didn't know what this had to do with me.

"You should be on my team," he said.

"Me?"

I saw Hector looking at me sideways. It was a suspicious look, the kind you see on detective shows.

"You knew about urushiol," Scott said.

"Lots of people know about urushiol."

"Think about it," he said. "But you have to let me know by the end of the day. That's the deadline for the sign-ups." He said this as if I hadn't heard it on the morning announcements.

"Who else is on the team?" You needed three people. This was on the announcements, too.

"Me," he said. "Duh. That's it, so far."

"I know about old movies," Hector said.

Scott turned his head. "What else?"

"Top 40."

Scott nodded, like he was thinking this over. "Who was the eighth president?" he asked.

Hector counted on his fingers.

"Van Buren," he said.

"What's the first element on the periodic table?"

"Hydrogen."

Scott nodded again. "Not bad," he said. "Though not helpful, because I knew those answers, too." He shrugged. "Okay. I'll take you both."

Hector and I talked it over after he left.

"Well, that was unexpected," I said. I noticed that Scott still didn't say anything about saving him from poison ivy.

"He didn't know about urushiol," said Hector. "Maybe he doesn't know about a lot of things. Maybe we should make our own team." He opened his fruit cup. "We could get Robert Scanlon." He held up the can, and then poured the juice and fruit into his mouth. Hector believed this saved on utensils.

Robert Scanlon was the smartest kid in seventh grade. Not that Hector and I were stupid or anything, but teachers asked Robert questions when they didn't know the answers. Robert would probably form his own trivia team.

I didn't think Hector and I would have much luck finding a third member better than Scott Dursky. While I was thinking about this, Hector reached his own conclusion.

"But I guess it would be weird if we did that," he finished. "I mean, form our own team without Scott."

"He asked us," I agreed. This was not something that usually happened to me—the being asked part. In PE, for example, I was never picked until near the end. It's not like I sucked at sports or anything. People made certain assumptions when they saw me because I am Chinese and Jewish. At the beginning of the year, the PE teacher, Mr. Multer, announced that I could be team captain if we were playing Ping-Pong; I pretended to laugh when everyone else did, but I was actually pretty steamed about it.

"I just don't get why Scott asked us," said Hector. "He could ask anyone."

"He asked us because we know stuff," I said. "Plus, we saved his butt."

Hector put the end of his backpack strap in his mouth and chewed on it. This is what he did when he wanted to think. "You know what?" he said. "Why not?"

Actually, I had a few reasons why not.

One was that it meant I'd have to answer questions in front of an audience of people. As someone who got flustered around certain attractive girls, this was not a comforting thought.

On the other hand, it was a chance to show certain attractive girls that I knew about stuff besides poison ivy. It was a chance to be on a team. It wasn't baseball (I made the first cut, but not the final), but it was something.

So at the end of the day, when I saw Scott Dursky standing next to his locker, I walked right up to him.

"Okay," I said. "We're in."

"Great," said Scott. "We're team 5."

"Wait," I said. "You already signed us up?"

"I knew you'd say yes."

"How?" I hadn't known I'd say yes.

"I know many things," Scott said. "That was just one of them."

I had to admit, Hector's question about why Scott

chose us bothered me more than I wanted it to. Coming to junior high last year was hard, because suddenly there was this pecking order, and Hector and I were not at the top. Or the middle. Scott was one of the more popular kids at school. He was tall, which seemed to be one of the keys to junior high popularity. One month into the school year, he set a new school record for running the mile, and he was one of the first kids to get his own Atari game system last year. (Apparently, his allowance was higher than mine. Or maybe his grandmother gave him actual money for his birthday, instead of velour sweatshirts.) He had a Members Only jacket, which my parents said was too expensive for a (hopefully) about-to-have-a-growth-spurt boy. And he had his own group of people to hang out with. A large group of people.

Hector and I did not have a large group of friends. It was just me and Hector, because a lot of kids found Hector a little strange. I kind of understood—Hector was a bit like a little old man, maybe because he spent so much time watching black-and-white movies with his grandmother. For instance, in the gym before school, Terry Sutphin (before he got poison ivy) was showing us this break-dance move called the worm. He lay on the floor and sort of rippled backward in a big wave.

"Pretty good," I said.

"Not bad," said Hector. "But you know who can really dance? Gene Kelly."

Terry jumped up from the floor, breathing a little hard. "Who's that? Is she hot?"

"Gene Kelly is a man," Hector said. "And he can dance. Have you ever seen *Singin' in the Rain*?"

I knew what *Singin' in the Rain* was—it was an old movie with a bunch of people singing (duh) in the rain (double-duh). Sometimes Hector needed a filter, like in a fish tank, to help keep the gunk out of the conversation. Terry looked at Hector out of the corner of his eye. Then he shook his head and walked away.

I wanted to give Hector a shove, but instead I just stood there, smiling idiotically, because Hector has been my friend since second grade. The rest of the morning in the gym— and the mornings after that—no one came to talk to Hector, and by extension, me. I guess they thought we didn't have much to say.

I figured one way to make more friends would be to become friends with popular people, which was another good reason to join Scott's trivia team. When he nominated himself captain, I agreed, even though I was pretty sure Hector would have voted for me. And when Scott suggested that we all come over to my house to practice trivia and watch movies the Sunday before the contest, I agreed. My parents always insisted that you should never invite yourself to other people's houses. But I pretended not to notice. "Yeah, that's a great idea," I said.

We had been practicing together during lunch and on our own, but it seemed like a good idea to try to get a longer practice in. My parents normally didn't let me have friends over on Sunday nights, but it was the week of Thanksgiving, and the teachers wouldn't be giving us much homework because kids were starting to head over the river and through the woods to wherever their grandmothers lived. But mine were close by. Wai Po actually lived with us. I hoped she would behave.

Wai Po was my mom's mom, on my Chinese side. She moved in with us because she got kicked out of her old apartment. She wouldn't tell us why, except that the management was *totally unreasonable* and that *I was happy to leave anyway*. I think it probably had something to do with her dog, Bao Bao, because he was yappy and has already destroyed two pillows and an ottoman since moving in with us. Bao Bao was a Lhasa apso. His name was pronounced like the *bow* in "bowwow" and it meant "treasure" in Chinese. It should have meant hairy, spoiled mop.

Wai Po only liked Chinese food, but Dad said we could order pizza when Scott and Hector came over. He was happy to have an excuse to order pizza because we've only been eating Chinese food since Wai Po arrived. We decided on the double cheese, but the pizza place screwed up and instead we got something called "Hawaiian pizza." Maybe ham and pineapple are popular in Hawaii (last state to join the union, in 1959) but to me, meat and fruit did not belong together. To me, fruit was fruit and meat was meat. It was wrong to mix them. Did you put bananas on meat loaf? Did you sprinkle blueberries on a drumstick? No. But then again, some people thought being Chinese and Jewish were two things that didn't belong together, and here I was: David Da-Wei Horowitz. I might be the only person in the whole world with that name.

"Good thing we don't keep kosher," said Dad when he opened the boxes and saw what was inside. We were too hungry to wait for a replacement.

Hector, who knew about my generally pizza-less existence, put a slice of pizza on a plate and walked over to Wai Po. "Mrs. Lin," he said. "Would you like to try a piece of Hawaiian pizza? It's really quite delicious."

Up to this point, Wai Po had pretty much refused all non-Chinese food, but Hector had a way with old ladies. Wai Po smiled and reached for the plate. She took a small nibble of the pizza.

"Finally, some American food with flavor," she said,

taking another bite. She finished the slice and then she fed the crust to Bao Bao. It was a certified miracle.

"We can finally start ordering pizza again," I said to Hector in a low voice. "You're a lifesaver."

Hector grinned. "You owe me."

I was already dreaming about future pizzas. Maybe we could even get pepperoni. But that was down the road. In the present we were stuck with Hawaiian. Scott picked off the pineapple pieces and flicked them at me and Hector. I also picked off the pineapple pieces, but I could still taste the juice on the pizza, ruining everything. That left me with just the salad. I poured on a bunch of extra Bac-O bits, which, despite the name, didn't contain any actual bacon.

Then Mom walked in with Lauren, who was wearing her Walkman and singing under her breath. As soon as Mom saw the pizza boxes, her lips got kind of puckered, like we'd gotten lemons as a topping instead of the pineapple.

"You ordered *pizza*?" she said to Dad. "We have leftovers in the fridge."

"Honey, David has his friends over. They don't want to eat our leftovers," said Dad.

Lauren pulled off her headphones and grabbed a slice of pizza.

"What button are you wearing?" asked Hector. Lauren had a large collection of buttons and she wore a different one each day. She was actually known for them at school. I didn't know where she got them all, but it didn't seem fair that she was a grade younger than me and was already known for something. I was not known for anything.

"You can't wear buttons while you play basketball." Lauren said this like Hector, who didn't play sports, would have no idea this was the case. "But I have one on my duffel bag." She held up her bag to show us a button with a picture of E.T.

"Cool," Hector said.

Lauren turned around and looked at my dad, who was still talking to my mom. "My team won tonight," she said. "If anyone cares."

"That's great," said Dad. Then to Mom: "A couple of pizzas will not put us in the poorhouse."

Mom forced a smile. "Lauren played very well. She scored six points." Then she said to Dad, "We're on a budget, remember? For your son's bar mitzvah? We could have put stamps on the invitations with that pizza money. Did you pick up that extra shift for next week?" Even though Dad had been Jewish twice as long as Mom had, Mom was doing most of the planning.

"Thanks for caring," said Lauren. She turned and ran upstairs to her room. When she slammed the door, it sounded like a firecracker.

Dad didn't say anything, which meant no, he hadn't gotten an extra shift. I tried to jump in and help him. "They sent us the wrong pizza anyway. Wai Po even likes it. And, um, there are some pieces left over." Don't ask me why I thought that was a helpful thing to say.

Mom shook her head. "That's just great," she said, though she obviously meant that it was the opposite of great. She turned to Dad. "Come help me in the living room." I knew that was an excuse to talk in private, because there was nothing anyone could possibly need help with in our living room.

My parents have tried to save up for my bar mitzvah, in some form or another, for the last couple of years. But now that my bar mitzvah was getting close, I didn't think they had saved enough. I told them that I didn't need anything fancy, but my dad said that my only job was to study hard and give a good speech; their job was to foot the bill.

When they fought, though, I wanted to do more, especially since I was not destined to be a Talmudic scholar or anything. I wanted to give a good speech or even a great speech, for my dad. But, like always, I was never sure what to say, particularly to a roomful of people who thought that thirteen was an age where you should have mastered the English language enough to be able to impart humor and wisdom at the very same time. After my parents left the room, Scott, Hector, and I went into the basement so we could practice trivia and so that we didn't have to listen to my parents fighting.

I pulled out our Trivial Pursuit game, which was more fun than reading through the *World Almanac*. Plus, I was betting at least half of the questions from the librarian would be taken off Trivial Pursuit cards. Scott pointed his finger upstairs. "World War III, huh?"

"It's not that bad," I said. "They'll get over it."

Scott shrugged. "Unless they don't. Your mom looked pretty mad."

"David's parents are okay," said Hector. "Let's just play."

We set up the board. "As captain," Scott said, "I should get an additional pie piece." In Trivial Pursuit, you have to fill your playing piece with wedges from the six different categories in order to win. We called them pie pieces because they looked like multicolored slices of pie.

"As captain," I said, "you get nothing. If anything, you should have to earn an extra pie piece."

My favorite part of the game was when one question connected to another; it was like learning about the world in pieces until you got a big chunk of knowledge. For example: The name Pennsylvania came from William Penn and the Latin word for woods, *silva*. King Charles of England gave William Penn the land to pay off a debt to Penn's father and called it *Pennsylvania* for "Penn's woods."

When we practiced with Trivial Pursuit cards, sometimes one question gave the answer to another question on the same card. Scott, for example, drew the Entertainment question *Who portrayed US Nazi leader George Lincoln Rockwell in* Roots II?, and just under it, in the History category, the question was *Who founded the American Nazi Party?*

"I don't know," said Scott. "Adolf Hitler, Junior?"

That got a laugh from Hector, but I felt weird about it. Being Jewish will do that to you with the Nazi questions.

Scott drew another question, in Geography, and directed it to me, about the location of Dam Square.

It sounded European but other than that, I wasn't sure. "Berlin?" I guessed.

"In a dam circle," joked Hector.

"Amsterdam," said Scott. "Get it? Amster*dam*, *Dam* Square?"

Then the next question asked for the author of Winnie-the-Pooh.

"Easy," said Hector. "Winnie-the-*Butt* makes Winnie-the-*Poo*."

"That's it," said Scott, tossing his pizza crust into the box. "I'm done. Let's watch the movie."

It had taken us forever to pick something out when Dad took us to the video store. I could always think of lots of things I wanted to watch when I wasn't at the video store, but as soon as I walked in, I forgot all the titles. We had finally picked out *Firefox*, a Clint Eastwood movie about stealing a plane from the Russians.

Unfortunately, we had failed to notice that we grabbed the VHS version of *Firefox*. Our VCR only used Betamax, the other kind of tape. I punched the power button to turn off the VCR and ran my fingers over the front where it read VIDEOCASSETTE RECORDER. It should have said VERY CRUMMY RECORDER.

"What kind of idiot gets Beta?" Scott grumbled. "You get longer recording time on VHS."

"Beta has a better picture," I said, repeating what my Dad had said when he had brought it home. This was a less compelling argument without an actual movie to prove my point.

Scott flipped through our four TV channels.

Channel 20 was showing reruns of *Green Acres*. NBC was showing *Manimal*, about a guy who could turn into different animals. CBS had a news special on unemployment.

"Only ABC left," Scott said. "This is our last chance."

The image on the television jumped and changed. "SAC, Omaha, Nebraska."

"That's Strategic Air Command," Scott said. A man, a general, walked through a huge plane.

"I knew that," I said. "About SAC."

"Remember it for the trivia contest."

"Hey, I know what this is," Hector said. "It's *The Day After*. We talked about it in history. It's about what would happen in a nuclear war. Little kids aren't supposed to watch and you're not supposed to watch *alone*."

Scott raised an eyebrow. "We're not alone, and we're not little kids." It was like he was daring us.

I didn't want to watch. The movie sounded serious, and I didn't want to be serious. But I wasn't going to be the one to say no, especially not in front of Scott. "Sure," I said. "Let's watch."

"They really did look like mushrooms," Hector said

when the movie was over.

"Well, of course, you dope. They didn't get their name because they look like cantaloupes," said Scott.

The Day After spent a long time showing nuclear weapons going off. At first, there was just a quiet *boom* and the cars and radios stopped working. And then you thought, *Well, that's not so bad.* But then the mushroom clouds rose up and for a few minutes it was all explosions and screaming and X-rayed skeletons where people had been a second before. They were usually running when they died.

"How could they not know what was happening?" I asked. That was one of the most upsetting parts. Some people knew to be scared, and other people didn't know they were supposed to be scared until they saw a missile go up. I didn't know what was worse: to have time to be scared, or not.

Scott shrugged. "There was all sorts of information. It was just a question of who you believed."

"I don't know anyone in Kansas, do you?" asked Hector. That's where most of *The Day After* took place. I'd never been to Kansas, but when they showed all the people running around, getting groceries, and trying to hide in basements, I felt sorry for them. They could be people from anywhere. The only creatures that seemed impervious to the radiation were the cockroaches.

"It's a made-up movie," said Hector.

"But there really *are* missile silos in Kansas," said Scott.

"And there really *are* nuclear weapons," I added. I had thought about nuclear war a lot, but I never thought about it the way the movie showed it—the way people died or got ugly and mean and sick. Mostly I'd thought about it the way they showed it in movies like *War Games*—like something that could happen if we weren't careful, but something we could avoid if we were. Now it didn't seem like we'd be able to avoid it at all, even if we were smart.

"Do you think the part about people losing their teeth and hair is true?" asked Hector. He always carried a black comb in his back pocket and he wore his hair kind of swooshy, like David Hasselhoff, which was something you couldn't do with hair that was part Jewish and part Chinese (but mostly Chinese).

"*That* part is true," Scott said. "Nuclear radiation isn't a beauty treatment."

"Well, what about the Russian girls?" Hector asked. "They'd still be pretty, right?"

"You'd go out with some Commie chick?" Scott reached over and whacked Hector on the head with a sofa pillow. He hadn't been hanging out with us very long, but the way he whacked Hector, it felt as if he had.

"You'd have to learn Russian," I pointed out.

"Not if you speak the language of love." Hector was joking. I think. "We could take another correspondence course," he added.

"I wouldn't do it," said Scott. "I'd rather die with honor." This was easy for Scott to say—he'd already had two girlfriends while the number of girlfriends Hector and I had added up to a grand total of zero.

I tried not to think about Kelli Ann Majors.

"Girls are just not that helpful. Now or during a nuclear war," Scott said.

"It probably won't happen," said Hector. "That'd be crazy, right?"

Scott shrugged. "The Soviets shot down that airplane full of civilians, didn't they?" Right before school started, the Russians shot down a Korean Airlines flight that had strayed into Soviet airspace. The Soviets said they thought it was one of our spy planes. The Russians eventually gave back some shoes that had washed up from the flight. They showed them on TV. Some of the shoes belonged to little kids.

"It's a long way from shooting down one airplane to blowing up an entire country," I said. "Right?"

"Well, I've got good news." Scott stood up and pointed out the tiny basement window. "We live ten miles from the capital of the United States. If the Russkies hit first, we're going to be like those people in the movie and get a one-way trip to the X-ray room." He smacked his hands together. "BAM. We won't even know what hit us."

This did not sound like good news to me.

"President Reagan wouldn't let that happen," Hector said. He ran his hand over the red carpet so that the path changed color and looked lighter. "He'd press the button first, right?"

"The Russians pushed the button first," I said. "In the movie."

"Well, that's my next point," Scott said. "Since both sides know that an attack from one side automatically brings about an attack from the other, no one will do it. That's what's supposed to keep any of it from happening." He enunciated his next words carefully. "It's called 'mutually-assured destruction.'"

I couldn't help noticing that the first letters in "mutually-assured destruction" spelled m-a-d. And mad can either mean "angry" or "crazy." Or both.

"So," said Hector. "The good news is the leaders of the two world superpowers are playing a game of nuclear chicken in which they'll never press the button. And if they do, the good news is that we'll be vaporized before we know it?"

"Pretty much," Scott said. "That's why they showed the movie. To remind us."

"Or to prepare us," I said. Nuclear war was on my list of things I knew probably wouldn't happen but could: forgetting to wear pants to school, getting my leg chomped off by a shark at Virginia Beach, sneezing on Kelli Ann if I tried to talk to her during gym. Now that nuclear war seemed like a real possibility, it was front and center, competing with—and now beating—my bar mitzvah speech for the title of Thing I Am Most Worried About.

The next day, everyone was talking about *The Day*

After at school. Lots of kids said they couldn't sleep, and the ones who could said they had nightmares. One girl even got sent to the clinic because she started crying about it and couldn't stop. Every time I was near a window, I looked at the sky, checking for signs of a nuclear war. On the way home from school, I heard a boom and an echo. I froze and thought *bomb* before I thought *garbage truck*. That was when I realized I needed a way to keep doing regular life stuff while still being aware of what might happen.

I decided that if the Soviet Union was going to attack us, it would be on a Tuesday.

I had some almost scientific reasoning for this. My dad had told me that the emergency room was the busiest on Mondays, because people call in sick and then they need a note for work. That got me thinking that there were probably days the Russians were more or less likely to attack. They wouldn't do it on a Friday—no one should attack on a Friday because you had the weekend to look forward to. And why screw up a perfectly good weekend on the planet by attacking on Saturday or Sunday?

That left Monday, Tuesday, Wednesday, and Thursday. My mom said that people at her office had a hard time getting started on Mondays. No one had any energy and the coffee machine was always broken. If you were going to make a huge decision like blowing up the world, you'd need a lot of energy and coffee. So that ruled out Monday. And everyone called Wednesday "hump day" because once you got over that day, you were headed toward the weekend. And who wouldn't want to hang on until the weekend? And Thursday was even closer to the weekend.

That left Tuesday. Tuesday was always the busiest day at my house. If Mom was going to work late, it was usually a Tuesday, and even though Dad had different shifts, he always ended up working on Tuesdays. My teachers gave the most homework on Tuesdays. Lauren and I usually had Hebrew school and then I met with the rabbi on Tuesdays (except for this week, when it was canceled).

If there ever was a day when ending life as we knew it seemed like an option, it would be a Tuesday.

My theory was confirmed even further the next day, when Eisenhower Junior High held its first trivia contest. That was a Tuesday, and it did, in fact, change life as we knew it.

Here's a question:

What's the difference between a seventh grader and an earthworm? Every once in a while, earthworms get respect. When Hector and I had thought about who we could have on a trivia team, we never even considered any eighth graders. There was no point; we were beneath them. There were three teams of eighth graders at the contest. I could overhear them, sizing up everybody else.

"They've got Finch—he'll be killer on the science questions."

"Yeah, except I heard he's not really good at chemistry; he just knows the periodic table. And look at them. They've got Margaret Medina. She reads all the time."

We, on the other hand, didn't even get discussed. Not even Robert Scanlon's team did. It's like we were just something that had to be dealt with and moved over. Like earthworms in the dirt.

It sounded corny, but after practicing together, I realized that Hector, Scott, and I had specialties, kind of like one of those military adventure movies, where everybody has a specialty that makes the whole operation work. Hector had a near-encyclopedic knowledge of 1940s and 1950s television shows and entertainers, thanks to his grandmother and reruns, and Scott knew every world and state capital. Scott also claimed to be something of a history scholar, but honestly, he just guessed Hitler or John F.

Kennedy on the history questions half the time, and got them right.

My specialty was sports and random information. The first NHL goaltender to be credited with a goal was Billy Smith with the New York Islanders. Siberian chipmunks camouflage their scent with snake urine. The average person farts fourteen times a day.

According to the rule sheet that Scott gave us, the questions were going to come from multiple sources including, but not limited to, the *World Almanac*, newspapers, the *Encyclopedia Britannica*, and Trivial Pursuit. You received ten points for each correct answer. You lost ten points for every answer you got wrong. The winner was the first team to get to three hundred points, but Mrs. Axelrod, the school librarian and moderator, had a twist for the end. "If you are about to reach three hundred points," the sheet read, "the team immediately behind you gets to select from which one of the following categories—Sports; Science; Art; Music, TV & Movies; US History; English; Math—your next question will come."

For most of the game, we were in third place, behind two of the eighth-grade teams. But then we hit a lucky streak, ten correct answers in a row, pulling into second place. One of the eighth-grade teams had their final question, and we picked Math.

Mrs. Axelrod opened the envelope and read the index

card inside. "*What system of measurement begins with six zeroes and ends with 235959?*"

I was stumped. It didn't even make any sense. If this was the type of math we were expected to know in eighth grade, I was in trouble. The eighth-grade captain shook his head. "Latitude and longitude?" he said.

"Incorrect. Another team may answer for ten points."

Ten points would get us to two hundred and ninety points. Hector raised his hand.

Math was not Hector's best subject. I didn't know why he was raising his hand. But before I could stop him, Hector said, "That's military time."

Mrs. Axelrod said, "That's correct. I would have also accepted the twenty-four-hour clock." She shuffled the envelopes. "Since you have reached two hundred ninety points, the other team will select the next question for you."

The pimply captain of the eighth-grade team looked at us like the fish bait that we were. "You guys have been missing science questions all day. We'll pick Science."

Mrs. Axelrod opened the envelope. "Final question for the seventh-grade team, in the subject of Science. *What is the sum total of eyes, ears, and noses on a common garden earthworm?*"

The audience, made up mostly of team alternates, parents, and some kids waiting for the late bus, began whispering.

I couldn't believe it. I'd memorized key British monarchs and rivers in China, but somehow, despite our similar lifestyles, earthworm anatomy had gotten by me.

Hector leaned in. "I think it's one of those super-obvious answers. They probably have two eyes, two ears, and a nose like everyone else."

Scott closed his own eyes. "Shh. I'm trying to think." He had a thin mustache, and when he thought about questions, he liked to run his fingers over it. I did not have a mustache, but I also didn't have pimples, so maybe it was a trade-off.

"Thirty seconds," said Mrs. Axelrod.

Sometimes, you knew the answer right away, and there was no better feeling. You knew the right thing to say and you just said it. It was trickier when you didn't know the exact answer, but instead you knew the range of *possible* answers. Then you had to start using the information you had on hand and work with your teammates. All I could think of was that book, *How to Eat Fried Worms,* where a kid ate a worm every day for fifteen days to win a bet. I loved that book in fourth grade, but I didn't remember any reference to worm eyeballs. I didn't remember anything about aural or visual perception. What did worms really have to perceive besides dirt?

Then it occurred to me—*maybe they didn't have eyes at all.*

"Fifteen seconds."

And if they had noses, they'd just be breathing dirt, so

they probably didn't have one of those, either. I debated whether I should say something. I was a great fan of the quote *It's better to be thought a fool than open one's mouth and prove it.*

Scott looked at me. "You got anything?"

No eyes, I thought. I opened my mouth, which I knew an earthworm did have, because they ate one third of their body weight in dirt every day. But nothing came out.

"I need an answer, please," said Mrs. Axelrod.

It's just a dumb contest, I told myself. Except for the people in the library, no one in the school probably even knew about it. But I wanted to win. I wanted to show the eighth graders that we hadn't made it on easy questions, that we were a team to be reckoned with and analyzed. And ideally, I wanted to be the guy with the right answer.

Under the table, Hector held up five fingers.

"The sum total is . . . zero," said Scott. He stroked his mustache. "Earthworms don't have eyes, ears, or noses."

Mrs. Axelrod looked at her index card. For a librarian, she sure did read slowly. "That answer is correct," she said.

I was right! That is, I would have been right, if I'd said anything. For a second, we were all quiet. Then Hector screamed, "We did it! We did it!" and we jumped up and down like maniacs.

Scott threw Mrs. Axelrod's remaining index cards up in the air as part of the celebration. They fell like confetti.

"Clean those up right now or you'll be disqualified," Mrs. Axelrod said. She made a face like someone had just used one of their fourteen farts, only nobody had.

"How did you know?" I asked Scott as we crawled under the table to pick up the cards. "About the earthworm."

Scott tugged out a card that had slid under a chair leg. "I kept saying in my head, *Earthworm eyes. Earthworm ears. Earthworm nose.* None of that sounded right. Where would the nose even go? And I thought maybe it was because there were no such things."

Then I *really* wished I'd spoken up. At least I had a reason for thinking what I did.

"But you could do that with anything," I said. "Like, *cricket knees, cricket knees.* Or *spider teeth.* And those exist."

Scott shrugged, but now I was all worked up again. This way, it didn't seem like we won because of our knowledge; we just won because of dumb luck. And then Scott got all the credit.

"Well done," said Dad. He shook our hands, like we'd just landed on the moon or something. "Way to get that last question, Scott."

Hector's parents and his little brother, Alonso, came over to congratulate us. "The trivia winners!" said Mr. Clelland. "Our smart boy." He put his arm around Mrs. Clelland and squeezed her. The Clellands were what my mom called *lovey-dovey.* Scott rolled his eyes.

"With smart friends," added Mrs. Clelland. "They've

been practicing with the Trivial Pursuit Genius Edition, you know."

The front of the Trivial Pursuit box actually said *Genus Edition,* but I didn't correct her. Mrs. Clelland was not the first person to make that mistake.

"Hello, Ben," Mr. Clelland said, shaking my father's hand. "I'd forgotten you were a doctor. Did you come straight from work?" Dad was still wearing his scrubs from his hospital shift.

I kind of hoped that Dad would just let the comment go by this time, but he didn't. "I'm a nurse, actually. Operating room."

"Ah," said Mr. Clelland. His smile became a little frozen. "A nurse." Not for the first time, I wished my dad was in a slightly more manly profession. Like lumberjack.

"Where are your parents, Scotty?" asked Mrs. Clelland. Hector, Scott, and I cringed, collectively. Scott is not a *Scotty.*

"Working, I guess," he said.

Mrs. Clelland nodded, though you could tell she thought they should have taken off work. She didn't miss anything that had to do with Hector and Alonso, up to and including Picture Day at school.

The eighth-grade team that came in second came over and shook our hands. "Congratulations. Not sure I would have gotten that last one," said the captain. That was a reward in itself—getting some recognition from the eighth graders, even if it was in that forced, good-game way, like in gym. Another reward: We'd have our names read over the announcements.

"Nice going, Scott," Mrs. Axelrod said as we filed out. "Good luck at the county contest. It's in January."

I hadn't known there was a next level of competition, but I smiled like I had known all along. My mind raced. If we won at county, that would be even better than beating the eighth graders. We would probably get in the school newspaper. We would be presented with certificates at a school-wide assembly, which would definitely help our status. There might even be a trophy, and Kelli Ann would see us get it. I pushed that last thought away, trying not to get too excited. I just had one other question about the date.

"It's not January twenty-first, is it?" I asked.

"I think it's earlier than that. I'll check. Big day, Mr. Horowitz?"

"You could say that."

For the last year, I've had a pretty good idea of what

I was going to be doing on January 21, 1984: being bar mitz-vahed in front of about a zillion people. This was pretty funny to me, since I could barely start a book report more than a day before it was due. But I'd known for a year that the twenty-first was the day I was supposed to read from the Torah and become a man.

So far, my body hadn't figured out the man part, though. I was the seventh-shortest person in the class (that included the girls) and while I had armpit hair (and a little BO) I didn't have any leg hair. Also, I really wanted the salespeople who phoned our house to stop calling me "ma'am."

I didn't expect to spring into a fully formed adult when I had my bar mitzvah, though it would be nice to have *some-thing* that showed I had this adult thing down. When my dad had his bar mitzvah, his voice cracked right in the mid-dle of his Torah reading and everybody laughed, nicely. Dad said that instead of feeling embarrassed, he laughed, too, which was kind of a sign of growing up, or at least feeling more comfortable in his own skin. Or voice box.

The congregation threw candy at him, and then he went out to lunch with his mom and dad and brother and grandparents and his neighbor, Mrs. Levine. I'd always hoped that my bar mitzvah would be like that, because we lived in Virginia and not in New York, where bar mitzvah celebrations were like Ringling Brothers. But when Granny M, my dad's mother, moved into our neighborhood, that changed in a hurry.

"Oh no," she said, in a voice that suggested I had asked for ham and cheese sandwiches at the reception. (Ham and cheese sandwiches were as non-kosher as you could get, and even though we didn't keep kosher, serving them at the reception—in Granny M's mind—would be a pretty huge mistake.) "That's not how it's done these days." You would think that she would be flattered that I wanted to do things the same way she'd done them for my dad, but she prided herself in keeping up with the times, even if all of the changes were not for the better.

After she said that, Granny M pulled out the tissue she always kept inside her sweater sleeve, and wiped a spot on the coffee table. My grandmother was slightly obsessed with germs, which was why she wanted a portable phone, even though they cost thousands of dollars. She thought pay phones were dirty.

But Granny M didn't spend a lot of time on the phone. She spent a lot of her time "popping in" to visit us. She moved into our neighborhood six weeks after Wai Po moved in. That was not a coincidence, in spite of what she might tell you.

Granny M had always been perfectly happy living in New York. She called it "the world center of culture." But when she heard that Wai Po was moving in with us, Granny M began to complain. She complained about the dirt and the noise and the traffic. They raised the price of subway fares. And wouldn't it be nice if we all lived a bit closer?

"Well, I'm afraid we're not moving," my dad said, which he thought would take care of everything. But he had underestimated the power of Granny M. She could have gone to live in San Diego, which was clean and which was where my uncle Josh, aunt Tracey, and cousin Ashley lived. But Granny M said that if she was going to move to the West Coast, she might as well move to China.

I don't think she meant anything by that.

Granny M (which was short for Marjorie) knew everybody. "You went to NYU dental school?" she'd ask a new neighbor who happened to be a dentist. "Do you know Dr. Grumman? He got his degree in '62. Where do you practice? Brooklyn?" She'd dig until she found some connection between that person and herself, either by synagogue or by the niece of her best friend's brother-in-law. It's what she called "Jewish Geography." If that were a trivia category, she'd win.

Anyway, it shouldn't have come as any surprise that shortly after Wai Po moved in, Granny M announced that she had a connection to our neighbors, the Dreightons. It turned out that Granny M's neighbor's son's colleague was none other than Harry Dreighton, aka Professor Harold Dreighton, around the corner from us. I had heard that the Dreightons were moving to Japan for a year for Dr. Dreighton's sabbatical, but Granny M had heard a lot more.

Such as the fact that the Dreightons were looking for someone to live in their house after the first renter dropped out at the last minute. Someone like their new friend, Marjorie Horowitz. She signed on the dotted line right away.

Ever since she moved in, Granny M had been trying to make sure my bar mitzvah was *done right*. This was because of her sister, Seal, which was short for Celia. They hadn't spoken in years, but for someone she didn't talk to, Granny M seemed to know a great deal about what her sister was doing. Seal just got back from a cruise. Seal got a new haircut. Most important, though, Seal's grandson, my cousin Jacob, had a bar mitzvah *done right*.

So now *done right* meant out-of-town guests, a hotel ballroom, and a new three-piece suit for me. Granny M asked me what I wanted as a party theme, which was also something Jacob had. I told her I knew what theme meant in my English class, but I didn't know what that meant for a bar mitzvah. I kind of hoped that that would deter her, but it only made her more excited.

"Do you like animals? Mitzi Shandler's granddaughter had an elephant at her bat mitzvah. And Gert's grandson's bar mitzvah was based on that movie, *Raiders of the Lost Ark*."

I didn't want an elephant or a giant rolling boulder at my party. I wasn't sure I wanted a party at all, since Mom and Dad were so worried about money. Up until Granny M took over, I was planning on only speaking in front of our congregation, and maybe Hector, and now, possibly Scott. My father kept saying things like "a compromise" and "something in between." But for Granny M, "in between" still involved official invitations. Plus, she said they had to be *engraved*, which made it sound like they would be made of gold.

My cousin Jacob had that, too.

On Tuesday evening, the night of our big victory, Granny M walked into our kitchen and Bao Bao let out a high-pitched bark, the canine equivalent of fingernails on a blackboard. It was his trademark.

"Can you get that dog to shush?" asked Granny M. "He sounds like a fire engine."

"He thinks you're an intruder," said Wai Po. "He's defending us." Wai Po put a little extra snap on the word *us*.

My mom tried to smooth things over. "I think Bao Bao is trying to welcome you! Bao Bao, hush."

Wai Po grunted into her tea. Bao Bao looked at Granny M, gave one last bark, and trotted out of the room as if he'd accomplished something.

"I got the invitations!" said Granny M, taking a card out of her purse with a flourish. "I just brought one to show you."

Mom pulled down her glasses and looked at the invitation.

It was blue, the color I had picked, and simple, because my mother said simple invitations looked "clean," unlike my bedroom. There was a Jewish star at the bottom.

Please join us as our son, David Horowitz, is called to the Torah . . .

"What was the grand total?" my mother asked. She was still trying to decide if my grandmother's helping was actually helpful.

"Seventy invitations didn't come cheap," said Granny M. "But this is on me."

But all I could think about was *seventy invitations?!* If you multiplied that by the Yagers or the Rosmans, who had four kids plus two parents each, that would equal four hundred and twenty people. I could barely speak in front of two people. How could I speak in front of four hundred and twenty?

"That seems like a lot of invitations," I said.

"Some of those people will be your friends," said Mom.

"Do you have many Jewish friends?" asked Granny M.

"More like *any* Jewish friends," I said.

There were only four Jewish boys at my school, and even though we saw each other in Hebrew school, it's not like we talked very much. I was the only one who was half-Jewish and half-Chinese.

Lauren came into the kitchen. "Do I get to invite any friends?" She had on a button that said, EXPERIENCE IS WHAT YOU GET WHEN YOU DON'T GET WHAT YOU WANT.

"Well," said Mom. "This is David's bar mitzvah."

"So?"

"When you have your bat mitzvah, you'll invite your friends."

"That's so unfair." Lauren glared at Mom. "I'll bet you'll let David invite *his* friends to my bat mitzvah." Then she stomped out of the kitchen.

"What about girls? You should invite girls." Granny M said it like this was a rule.

There were only two Jewish girls at my school, who made up the rest of my Hebrew class. That was the only place I talked to them. In regular school I didn't talk to them at all. I was pretty sure Mom was going to say I had to invite them. The only girl I thought about inviting was Kelli Ann, because my grandmother kept insisting there would be dancing. My face turned red, I could feel it.

"I'll need a list," Granny M said. "If I'm going to hire a calligrapher."

"I'll think about it," I told her.

"Let me see the invitation," said Wai Po. She scrunched up her face while she read it. "Where is David's middle name? His *Chinese* middle name. It says David Horowitz. It has his name in English and Hebrew. Where is Da-Wei?"

Now Mom turned red. "I missed that completely." She said something to Wai Po in Chinese. I recognized the word *gui*, from when Wai Po went clothes shopping with us. It meant "expensive."

Wai Po scowled and answered in a short burst of rapid-fire Chinese. Judging from her tone and the length of her answer, I was willing to bet that she wasn't saying, *I am totally fine with what's going on and just want David to enjoy his bar mitzvah.* She picked up Bao Bao and left the room as Dad walked in.

"How's everything going?" asked Dad.

"Could be better," said Mom. "Ma just pointed out that we forgot to include David's middle name on the invitation." She waved the invitation at him, like a fan.

"I can't believe we missed that," said Dad. "Oh well, we'll just have to reprint them."

"So suddenly we're the Rockefellers?" said Granny M. "If we had a wrong address, maybe we'd reprint. If there was a mistake. But there isn't a mistake. Besides, the Chinese name is just more confusing."

It was a Tuesday, and the potential for World War III loomed above us.

"It sounds better with the full name," my mother said. "But you're right, Marjorie. I think we can manage without it." I wondered if Granny M had left out my Chinese name on purpose. I looked from Mom to Granny M to Dad. Was I supposed to say something like *that's okay*, so they wouldn't have to spend more money? But I wasn't sure if it *was* okay, so I didn't say anything. "Reprinting them would be a waste—of money and of resources." Mom sighed. "I'm not sure there will even be time to make new ones. I'll just explain things to my mother."

"Maybe we could hand-deliver the invitations so we could save on postage," I said. "Then we could explain when we give out the invitations."

"It's better to mail them," said Granny M. "That's doing it right."

"And expensively," muttered my mom. I don't think she meant Granny M to hear her say that, but Granny M gave Mom a look.

Mom gave her a look back.

Dad clapped his hands. "Speaking of doing things properly, we should talk about the Thanksgiving menu!" You could see that my dad was working hard to change the subject. He does that when things get uncomfortable.

"I've got the menu under control," said my mother. She tapped her head, where I guess the menu was written. Or engraved.

"I can make the turkey," said Granny M.

"That's so much work," my mother said. "I've got it."

"Psshht," said Granny M. "I've made a million of them. Besides, Ben loves the way I make turkey."

Mom looked at Dad and Dad shrugged. I thought Dad was pretty smart, not saying anything. "Well," said Mom. "I suppose that would free up the oven for the pies and casseroles."

Wai Po walked back in, this time with Bao Bao on a leash. "We are going for a walk," she said stiffly.

"We're talking about Thanksgiving," said Mom. She was trying to act like everything was okay. "Is there anything special you want me to add to the menu? Marjorie said she would make the turkey."

"Turkey is so dry," said Wai Po as she and Bao Bao marched to the door. "What about a nice Peking duck?"

After Wai Po made her Peking duck comment, there was a whole discussion of The Proper Foods to Bring to Thanksgiving. Granny M kept saying that we had to stay traditional. Wai Po wanted to cook Chinese food. "I do not want my grandchildren to forget that they are Chinese," she said.

"*Part* Chinese," said Granny M.

The way they were talking, you'd think there was a dotted line dividing us into equal and separate halves.

"All foods are fine," said Mom. "It will be delicious." This only made both grandmothers unhappy.

That night I dreamed that my grandmothers became animated poultry carcasses. Wai Po was a roasted brown Peking duck and Granny M was a golden-yellow turkey. Granny M's turkey hit Wai Po's duck with a spatula, while Wai Po's duck fought back with a pair of chopsticks. Then a timer went off and they both exploded.

When I woke up, I started worrying that my grandmothers would get into a fistfight at the synagogue in front of everyone I knew, including Kelli Ann. If I invited her. It was a scary enough thought that I studied for my test on the Industrial Revolution, even though it wasn't for another week.

My school, Dwight D. Eisenhower Junior High, was originally built for five hundred kids. There were now seven hundred and fifty-two of us, which meant things were kind of crowded. If you were in seventh grade, you had to share a locker, and lunch started at 10:42 so that all the kids had a chance to eat. Trying to get to class felt like swimming upstream, while every other fish in the river swam downstream, straight at you.

Usually, I spotted Kelli Ann within the first ten seconds of the end of second period, and then I had to pretend not to see her while heading in her direction. But today I was so busy thinking about my weird dream that I really *didn't* see her until the crowd practically pushed us together.

"Oh, hey." Short but friendly and a little cool, with a bit of a chin lift. Yes, I'd been practicing for this moment, to say just the right thing, in just the right way.

Kelli Ann looked at me and smiled. "Hey, David." She pulled her hair around her neck so that it was all on one side. Her hair was wavy and the color of caramels, which used to be one of my favorite candies until I got braces. "What's up?"

"Not much." Uh-oh. I hadn't counted on having a conversation with Kelli Ann. "Um, are you theady for Ranksgiving?"

Kelli Ann wrinkled her very cute nose at me. "What?"

Here is my one contribution to the betterment of humanity: When someone doesn't hear you clearly the first time, *don't repeat exactly what you just said.* It just gets more confusing, because the other person's brain has already messed up that sentence pattern. Say what you want to say, but a little differently.

"Ready for a long weekend?" I said.

Kelli Ann shrugged. "I'm spending it with my dad, which means we're spending it with his new girlfriend." She always looked so happy that I assumed her life was perfect. I wasn't sure what to say when I found out it wasn't. I decided to agree with her. That was pretty safe.

"That stinks," I said. "Sorry."

Kelli Ann shrugged again, and I wondered if I made a mistake, saying that her life stunk. If someone ever wanted to make a helpful version of Trivial Pursuit, they would create a How to Talk to Girls category. *What should you say to a girl when you have fifteen seconds to talk?* Unfortunately, I ended up smiling idiotically (*Your life stinks! That's great!*), and watching Kelli Ann slide away to the girls' locker room door.

_____

In PE, we had to wear a gym suit, which was really not a suit, just a yellow T-shirt and blue shorts. I guess the school wanted us to be easy to spot in case anyone tried to flee the grounds.

I left the locker room and headed out to the field. Hector was already running laps. We usually had to do three at the beginning of PE and three at the end, which meant there wasn't a lot of time left for whatever activity Mr. Multer chose for the day. If you ask me, he planned it that way. I caught up to Hector so we could talk, even though he was a lap ahead of me. Kelli Ann wasn't outside yet. The only girl running down the worn trail around the field was Joy Bachelder, who made it her personal goal to come in first, even though it wasn't a race.

"It's freezing," I said to Hector as we cut through the November air. "You want to do some trivia?" Running laps was a great time to practice trivia questions; it made the running less boring.

Hector nodded. He was breathing through his nose, which was what you were supposed to do to keep your throat from getting raw. I pulled out the *Pocket Book of World Trivia*, a book I'd gotten from the drugstore to carry around so that I would always be ready to practice. "*What is the official language of Quebec, Canada?*"

"They speak English in Canada, don't they?"

I flipped to the answer page. "But French is the official language of Quebec."

"*Zut alors!* Or however you say that in French. Gimme a movie one."

"*What was the first movie to show a toilet flushing?*"

"A toilet flushing? That's a weird one. Let me think." When we didn't know an answer, we tried to reason it out so we could make the best possible guess. "If it was the first, it was probably an old one," Hector said. "And a lot of old movies didn't even show bathrooms." We ran a few yards. "Wait! That Hitchcock movie with the shower scene. *Psycho.*"

I checked the answers. "Correct!" That was some pretty good deducing. I tried not to trip over my feet as I scanned other questions in the same chapter, marked Amusements. "*What famous cartoon character was almost named Mortimer?*" I asked.

"Ummm. Was it Casper the Friendly Ghost?"

"No, Mickey Mouse."

Hector laughed. "Mortimer Mouse. I don't think so. By the way, we're going to Walt Disney World for Thanksgiving." He said it like it was no big deal, because we're supposed to be too old to get excited about things like Disney World, but I could tell he really was. Hector's family went on a lot of these vacations, and he was excited every time.

"Cool." I tried to say it like I meant it, but it was hard to be happy for Hector in the Magic Kingdom when I was going to be stuck in the Land of Battling Birds. "When are you leaving?"

"Tonight." Hector started talking faster. "My parents have had it planned for a long time, only they didn't say anything until yesterday. I think they were going to keep it a secret until today. They only told us because my little brother was asking if ducks would lose their beaks after exposure to radiation."

"Your brother saw *The Day After*?" Alonso seemed awfully young to be worried about nuclear radiation.

"He heard me telling my parents about it, the part about the teeth," explained Hector. "I thought Alonso had gone to bed, but he was listening on the stairs. He does that."

"What do ducks losing their beaks have to do with Disney World?"

"After he heard us talking, he started crying and freaking out. My parents told him about Disney World to distract him," Hector said. "It almost worked, except now he keeps asking questions about the beaks of Disney ducks, like Donald and Daisy. And I keep thinking about the beaks of real ducks because Alonso has a point: If humans lose their teeth, ducks will probably lose stuff, too. Like feathers."

"Yeah," I said. "Feathers are always the first to go."

Hector finished his laps and I took my last one alone. Kelli Ann was running now, and I wasn't sure whether I should speed up and pass her so she could see how fast I was, or try to run beside her. Before I could decide, Mr. Multer called us in. I figured that meant we'd go inside and spend the rest of the time playing dodgeball. But when we headed back into the gym, Mr. Multer had a boom box plugged into the outlet. There wasn't a ball in sight.

"We already did our dance unit," Hector said, loud enough for Mr. Multer to hear. We did square dancing for a torturous two weeks; I spent most of my time counting people to figure out if I would get paired with Kelli Ann for the Virginia reel. We got paired once out of thirty-two possible times.

"We're not dancing," Mr. Multer said. He put a cassette in the boom box, which he must have brought from home; the school just owned record players that were centuries old. "We're doing aerobics." He clapped his hands. "Everyone find a spot and march in place!"

Mr. Multer hit play and we heard the drums from the beginning of the Go-Go's "We Got the Beat." I decided that I needed to be in the back of the room. A lot of guys stood back there, too. Then Mr. Multer told us to grapevine right, which meant to walk sideways while crisscrossing your legs. The girls moved in unison, as if they'd been practicing for months. Hector and I ran into each other.

"He said to go right," said Hector.

"I thought he meant *his* right." Apparently, I'd overthought it.

"This makes me miss square dancing," Hector said.

I would have agreed, except I had a clear view of Kelli Ann in the second row. She was next to Michelle, her best friend. They looked at each other and laughed a lot and their long legs didn't get tangled up in the grapevine. Kelli Ann's hair was in a ponytail, and, for a moment, I just watched it swing back and forth. That would be a good way to hypnotize junior high boys, not just me.

"Okay," yelled Mr. Multer. "Pivot turn!"

Suddenly, all of us who were cowering in the back row were at the *front* of the class. It was hard enough to try to figure out what Mr. Multer wanted us to do, but trying to do it in time to the music with the whole class (and Kelli Ann) watching was impossible.

By the time it was over, it was clear that I didn't have the beat and I was never going to get it. And I was never going to get a move Mr. Multer called the mambo cha-cha.

I was still trying to figure out the mambo cha-cha

and the V-step on the way to English, which might explain why I crashed into the door.

"Smooth," said Scott as I sat down next to him. I'd changed seats when we'd formed the trivia team so we could pass questions back and forth during class.

"Well!" said Mr. Haggerty, straightening his tie. He had the world's largest collection of knitted ties. They were bumpy and floppy, like Mr. Haggerty. "It's your last Thanksgiving before 1984."

Mr. Haggerty was mildly obsessed with the idea that we were going to read the book *1984* in the year 1984. It was as though he planned his whole career so he could make this joke, which was kind of sad. Then again, if there was a nuclear war, he'd be going out on top.

If you haven't read it yet: *1984* was written in the forties by a guy named George Orwell (Scott called him George

Bore-well) about a society in the distant future, also known as *right now*. According to Mr. Haggerty, who was supposed to be saving *1984* (the book) for 1984 (the year) but was giving everything away, the 1940s version of the 1980s was pretty bad. It depicted a never-ending war. The leader was a guy named Big Brother who may or may not exist, and he watched you all the time. Also, the book mentioned sex, which Hector's parents were very upset about.

Mr. Haggerty said that in the book, the future was scary.

The thing was: That future was right now, and now was scary, too.

My dad told me we had no idea what living in a scary world was really like. "Try hiding under your desk and pretending that it will save you if there's a bomb. That's what your mother and I did. Or what about the Cuban Missile Crisis? Did you learn about that yet?"

We learned about the Cuban Missile Crisis in Mr. Hudson's class, but the thing was, it didn't feel like things had gotten that much better. Just because the US and the Soviet Union were talking more than they used to didn't mean they were getting along. Someone could go too far at any moment. *The Day After* proved it. *War Games* proved it. The Korean jet at the bottom of the ocean proved it. All it took was the push of a button—it just wasn't that hard. Hadn't President Reagan called the Soviets the "Evil Empire"? And who even knew what they were calling us?

Mr. Haggerty spent most of the class showing *The Autobiography of Miss Jane Pittman*, which was based on a book about the past instead of the future. In spite of his lousy sense of humor, he was smart enough not to try to lecture about anything the last period before Thanksgiving break.

As the opening credits came on, I thought about what Mr. Haggerty said. What if this wasn't just the last Thanksgiving before 1984? What if the Russians pushed the button and this was the last Thanksgiving *ever*? What if my talk with Kelli Ann in the hallway was the only good conversation I'd ever have with her—or any other girl? What if *1984* ended up being the last book I ever read? What if I never got to become a man? Or what if I survived but ended up sick, with bad skin and no hair or teeth?

Scott leaned over. "Guess who I am," he said, then switched to a high-pitched voice, like a little kid. "'I'm going to Disney World with my mommy and daddy!'" Apparently he had talked to Hector, too.

I imagined the mushroom cloud hanging over the Magic Kingdom.

"It's one way to spend Thanksgiving," I said. Then I added, "If you're about five years old." As soon as the words came out of my mouth, I felt like a jerk. But Scott laughed.

"Hey, if you're going to be in town, you should come over after school today." Scott said this as a statement, not a request. He leaned in close.

"I have a *plan*," he said. "You'll want to be in on it."

After school, Scott and I walked together, but instead of going in the direction of his house, we went out to Stone Gate Drive, and then turned down a street that wasn't very developed. The houses were small, but on huge tracts of land. Scott walked up to a small tan house, and pointed to the field behind it. "There," he said. "We can dig back here."

"Dig what?"

"A fallout shelter," he said. "We're not getting toasted when the big bomb comes. We're going to be *survivors.*"

It took me a moment to absorb this idea.

"Won't the owner of the house mind?"

"Naw," said Scott. He waved his hand toward the field. "We own it."

This was news to me. Scott lived in Fox Run, one of the nicest subdivisions in our area. His house was huge. He could take in *two* grandmothers, no sweat.

"Really? Since when?"

Scott shrugged. "A while."

"What are your parents doing with a second house? Is this going to be a rental or something?" I almost said *vacation house,* but that was stupid. Why would Scott's parents buy a vacation house two miles from their regular house?

"Don't ask me to explain my parents," he said. He zipped up his jacket. "So, do you want to dig a fallout shelter, or not?"

It was strange, but the idea of digging a fallout shelter,

which was for a worst-case scenario, made me feel better. Maybe it's because I would actually be doing something. "Yeah, let's dig."

Scott paced off the different areas of the shelter. "One for you, one for me, and one for supplies." He made the shape of a star, with different arms coming off one main room.

"What about Hector?"

Scott didn't say anything for a minute. Then he reached into his backpack and pulled out a small shovel. He unfolded the handle with a click.

"Here's the thing," Scott said. "You have to be really careful who you invite into a shelter. The wrong person could bring you down or make you weak. See, like, I didn't even invite my own parents; I'm only talking to you. I don't know about Hector. He might not be strong enough. His parents make his life awfully easy for him."

That didn't seem fair. Hector actually had more chores than I did, and his parents expected him to get straight As. His dad was a marine. I wondered if I should point this out.

"My uncle was on a submarine, and they have to pass all these tests to see if they can take it, the time below the surface plus being in crowded quarters," continued Scott. "Some people get kind of nuts and we could be down there a long time. Only the strong survive."

While I didn't necessarily agree about Hector being weak, it was kind of cool to be the one friend Scott would pick. And the thing was, I *did* want in, which meant

59

agreeing, at least for now, with the guy whose family owned the property where we were digging.

"We can decide later," I said.

"If there's time," said Scott.

"We have at least until Tuesday," I said. When Scott gave me a strange look, I explained my theory, about how Tuesday was the only sensible day to expect an attack.

"I don't know how to break this to you," said Scott. "But history does not back you up on this. Attack on Pearl Harbor? Sunday morning. The beginning of the Korean War was also on a Sunday." Scott shook his head. "You're expecting these guys to be like us. They're not. They're going to be merciless, and we have to be tough."

I couldn't believe how quickly Scott had destroyed my argument. He was right, though—something terrible could happen at any minute.

"Let's just start digging," I said, trying to hide my expression.

"Don't freak out, though, okay?" said Scott. "*We* are going to be okay. We're doing something. We're going to survive."

What about Hector and everyone else? I wanted to ask. But there was also something reassuring in how confident Scott was. If I just did what he said, we'd be okay.

Scott held the shovel over his head. "To the fallout shelter!" he shouted. He handed me the shovel. I guess I had to yell something, too.

"To survival!" Then, to prove how manly I was, I

slammed the shovel blade into the earth. The blade went in about halfway.

"This is it," said Scott. "No going back."

I dug first, which was tough with the little shovel. Then I gave the shovel to Scott. Even though it was cold out, we both got sweaty. Also, it was hard to stay excited while you were digging a hole, which is why I pulled out my trivia book.

"Okay," I said. "*What country's secret police is known as the Stasi?*"

"East Germany." He didn't even look up.

"Too easy," I said, since I knew that one, too. I shuffled through the book until I found a trick question. "*Whose nickname means 'man of steel'?*"

"Superman, duh."

That's what I had thought until I read the question more carefully. "It doesn't ask whose nickname *is* the man of steel, it asks whose name *means* 'man of steel.'"

"I stand by my answer," said Scott.

"It's Stalin."

"Stinking Soviets. They tried to steal Superman's nickname." Scott punched the shovel down in the hole, a little harder than he needed to. "These questions are annoying. I'm trying to dig."

That kind of stung, especially since we had the county contest to prepare for, but I put the book away. We took a break for Coke and Funyuns, which Scott also had in his backpack. Then he handed the shovel to me.

When I got home, I left my shoes outside. Even if my mom hadn't had the no-shoes-in-the-house rule, I knew they were too muddy to wear inside. As far as I can tell, most Chinese homes have the no-shoes rule, though my dad is the one who loves walking around in his socks and asks my friends to take their shoes off.

Our house already smelled like Thanksgiving. I could smell cinnamon, apple, and pumpkin. And butter. There must be a part of your brain that's just for enjoying butter. But when I got to the kitchen, it didn't *sound* like Thanksgiving.

"I thought you were making a meringue." Granny M was standing behind Wai Po, who was whisking egg whites in a silver bowl. There was a *sk-sk-sk* of metal on metal.

"I am," said Wai Po.

"Then I'm confused," said Granny M, "because meringue is supposed to have peaks, like mountains. You're making valleys."

"I see a peak," said Wai Po. "You can't have valleys without peaks. Maybe you should have your vision checked. And you should check the apples on the stove. I think they are burning."

"Oh, don't worry about me. The only thing sharper than my vision," said Granny M, "is my sense of smell."

If the Soviets didn't blow us up, my grandmothers just might.

As I got cleaned up, I dissected my conversation

with Kelli Ann as if it was an earthworm. She'd shared something personal with me, about her parents' divorce. That had to mean something, even if I hadn't come up with anything intelligent to say back. Before that, the most personal thing I knew about Kelli Ann was that she had a Trapper Keeper with horses on it.

In science, Mrs. Osterberg had been teaching us about the scientific method, which is how scientists develop experiments. You had sections like Purpose (why you were doing the experiment) and Hypothesis (how you thought things were going to turn out). You also had to look at Independent Variables (things that changed), Dependent Variables (things that changed because of the Independent Variables), and Constant Variables (things that always stayed the same).

I thought about talking to Kelli Ann along the lines of the scientific method. My purpose was how to get Kelli Ann to think I was interesting. My hypothesis was that some sentences worked better than others. Kelli Ann thought I was interesting when I saved the seventh grade from poison ivy, but I was pretty sure that was a one-shot deal. Besides, Hector was there, so that didn't totally count. She also seemed to like talking about Thanksgiving. Maybe I was doomed to only talk to her about things that happened once a year. I knew lots of interesting trivia but it was sort of like what happened in the video store—as soon as I saw her, it all went out of my head.

When I was in fifth grade and we had to do this pen pal thing with a school out in Minnesota, our teacher told us we should ask questions when we didn't know what to say, because people liked to talk about themselves. But the only questions I could think of for Kelli Ann were *What makes you smell so good?* and *If I asked you to see a movie, would you say yes?*

The hard part was school, the constant variable in this scenario. There were always other people and other things to worry about. Who could think straight with all the pushing and noise and chatter? How was someone supposed to come up with something to talk about? Something *conversation-worthy.* And under a time crunch, too. Even Shakespeare wouldn't have been able to come up with all those lines— *To be, or not to be—that is the question*—if he had to walk from one end of the building to the other *and* dress for PE in two minutes.

If we were going to really get to know each other, it would

have to be somewhere private. Like a fallout shelter. Suddenly, I saw a small, possible upside to nuclear war: In a fallout shelter, it would be quiet. I could see us sitting side by side, Kelli Ann's head on my shoulder. I'd be able to smell her hair without moving my head—apple blossom shampoo—at least until the smell wore off and we couldn't take showers anymore. We could talk about our favorite movies and books. Maybe we'd even use some of our precious battery power to play music. Something soft and slow that didn't make you think of the mambo cha-cha.

We'd have all the time in the world. There'd be no interruptions.

It'd be great.

As I've said before, liking a girl does strange things to your mind. I was actually imagining a scenario where nuclear war wasn't a complete and total disaster.

It's not like we could get out of the hole right away. We'd probably have to stay in there for weeks until it was safe to come out. I would make her laugh when things got rough, and make her feel safe. It'd be my chance to be the greatest guy in the world, like the poison ivy thing, times a million.

Just me and Kelli Ann.

Except.

After a few weeks, I'd develop massive BO from not being able to shower. She wouldn't be able to shower, either, which might even things out, though I couldn't imagine Kelli Ann with BO. Ditto for teeth brushing. Kissing, even with equally gross mouths, was not an attractive option. The batteries for the radio would eventually die out, which meant no more music, which I was counting on to fill in any awkward moments.

Kelli Ann would probably end up wishing that she'd been zapped instead of having to hang out with me.

Okay—nix the nuclear-war-as-way-to-get-to-know-Kelli-Ann idea.

It would be better to try to get to know her under more civilized circumstances. Ones where I'd be decent-smelling and not too idiotic.

Preferably a place where I'd stand out and be noticed.

And maybe even a little manly.

Like my bar mitzvah.

We wouldn't be alone, but I'd have to spend time with her. Granny M had been really clear on that: "You'll have to make the rounds, David, and thank everyone for coming." And I'd know everyone there, except maybe some really old relatives, and I'd just have to pretend to know them, according to Granny M. I would be the center of attention—an idea both terrifying and appealing in its possibilities. Kelli Ann would have to notice me. She might want to dance with me. If I couldn't be the most popular guy at my own bar mitzvah, I should probably go live in a hole in the ground now.

All I needed was a killer speech, some great music to dance to, and two grandmothers who wouldn't embarrass me to death.

After dinner, Wai Po asked me to go for a walk with her and Bao Bao. I was going to say no, but then Mom gave me the raised eyebrow and mouthed *be nice*. I got my jacket.

Wai Po grabbed a white plastic bag and handed it to me. "For *da bian*," she said. Even though I don't speak much Chinese, I knew what *that* meant. Nobody else in our neighborhood carried a bag for *da bian*, but the apartments where Wai Po had lived were part of a planned community where it was required.

Sure enough, we were only a block away when Bao Bao squatted. I sighed and put the bag over my hand, but Wai Po grabbed the bag away from me.

"*Ai!*" she said in a scolding voice. "That's dirty!"

Well, yeah, I knew that. I was trying to be nice, picking it up for her. For a small dog, Bao Bao makes giant, bad-smelling poo.

Wai Po grinned and made a big show of putting the bag over her hand. Then she bent down and picked up a small brown object out of the neighbors' yard. Only it wasn't poo. It was a pinecone.

Wai Po flipped the bag inside out, twisted it closed, and handed it back to me. "*Da bian*," she announced, the same way you would say "ta-da!" Is that what she'd been doing all of these months? Carrying around a bag of pinecones? I had to admit, it was pretty brilliant. Anybody looking at her would think it was the real *da bian*. And anyone seeing the poop near the O'Dowds' bush would never think of blaming my grandmother. This was even better than the fake poop trick they sold at Spencer's—mostly because that poop cost $2.95, and the pinecones were free.

We walked a little farther. I took out another bag and picked up two more pinecones.

Wai Po smiled. "Bao Bao really had to go today," she said.

If only I had known this from the beginning, I wouldn't have complained so much every time I had to walk the dog.

I grabbed another pinecone and added it to the bag. "Do not overdo," Wai Po said. "That is the key. Bao Bao is a small dog."

Who knew Wai Po could be so sneaky? It actually made me appreciate her a little more.

"Wow, Wai Po," I said. "You have all sorts of hidden talents."

Wai Po laughed. "You don't know anything about your Wai Po. You think I'm just an old woman. But I was a beautiful girl. So many boyfriends! Your grandfather was lucky to get me." She smiled proudly. Then she added, "But I was also lucky." She held out her hand. "Even though we did not have wedding rings in China, your grandfather wanted me to have a ring when we came to the US." The ring on her hand was gold with a pearl and a ruby.

I knew the other story of the ring, the one my grandmother didn't like to talk about as much. My grandfather had decided to have the ring engraved with his name, but the engraver messed up his name. Instead of *Love, Shao Long*, the engraver had written, *Love, Shao Lom.* Instead of having it fixed, my grandfather told my grandmother that as long as she kept the ring on her finger, no one would see the mistake.

"When I die, Lauren will have it," she declared. "Now I only have Bao Bao, and you and Lauren. You are the apples in my eye."

I decided this was not a good time to correct Wai Po's English, even though multiple apples in the eye sounded kind of painful.

"Granny M says that Lauren will get her wedding ring, too," I said, hoping that Wai Po would see that she and Granny M were more alike than she thought.

Instead, Wai Po gave the leash a tug so we could head back home. "Amazing anyone married her," she grunted.

"You guys actually have a lot in common," I said. I put on my best grandson smile. "Including me."

Wai Po sighed. "David, do you know what *wai* in *wai po* means?"

Wai sounded sort of like *why*, but I knew that wasn't it. I shook my head.

"*Wai* means outside, like *waimian*," said Wai Po. "When the daughter gets married, she belongs to the husband's family, and the *wai po* is on the outside." I'd never heard of that. Granny M would probably argue that *she* was the grandma on the outside.

"That's in China, not here," I said.

"Your last name is *her* last name. You have a bar mitzvah, but you do not go to Chinese school. The family belongs to her," said Wai Po. "Even my own daughter is Jewish now. I have to work to keep my place, keep what's mine."

The closest Chinese school was an hour away and conflicted with Saturday-morning services, but I didn't think that was my best argument. "You live with us," I pointed out. "Granny M doesn't."

Wai Po nodded. "This is what I am talking about."

"Are you saying that you got kicked out on purpose so you had to live with us?" I joked.

She shrugged. I couldn't believe it. Wai Po had lived in a really nice place, with a swimming pool and a library and a huge garden. Mom always said that the grounds were "immaculate."

Then I looked down at Bao Bao, who was sniffing a fire hydrant. It all clicked together. "Did you get kicked out for picking up pinecones instead of Bao Bao's poop?"

"Except for that one time, they could not prove anything," Wai Po said.

"I invited Mr. Pickens to Thanksgiving," Mom
announced at breakfast. "He was going to spend
Thanksgiving with his son, but now his son has to work. I
couldn't let him be alone."

Mr. Pickens was a nice guy. He hosted a Fourth of July
barbecue for the neighborhood, and he used to pay me to
take in his mail and look after his dog, Rocky, when he went
out of town. Based on how my grandmothers started acting,
though, you'd have thought the president of the United
States was coming. When Granny M told Lauren to start
polishing the silver gravy boat, I decided that was my cue to
get out before they recruited me.

Dad was hiding out in the family room, watching TV.
Bao Bao was also in there, vigorously cleaning his butt. As
soon as Dad saw me, he turned down the volume, but not
before I heard a deep newscaster voice say, ". . . and the US

is still reeling from the Soviet walkouts. More news at six. Now back to the game."

"What was that?" I asked.

"Keep your voice down," said Dad. "I'm not supposed to check on the scores before dinner."

"No, but what did they say? Walk out from where? Geneva?" Now that the TV volume was off, Bao Bao's licking was really loud. *Glurp, glurp, glurp.*

"It's because the first parts of the cruise missiles just arrived in the UK," explained Dad. "The Soviets didn't want to have US missiles in Europe. They walked out of the disarmament talks." He glanced at the TV. "C'mon, St. Louis!" Dad wasn't really a Cardinals fan. He just wanted the Cowboys to lose.

Now we had all the elements of Thanksgiving: food, football . . . and imminent nuclear disaster.

"But is this *it*?" I thought I was going to be sick. Maybe the Soviets were walking out so they could go back to Russia and press the button. Just as Scott said, this would be a perfect day for them to attack, when everyone was fat and lazy from too much turkey.

"It's not the end of the world," said Dad. "C'mon, I could catch that!" He seemed more concerned about football than nuclear devastation. "They'll work something out, David," he added. "They always do." He turned off the TV and put his arm around my shoulders. I wasn't sure if he was talking about football or nuclear disarmament. "I think we've waited long enough. It's a good time to offer to help."

Bao Bao stood up and wagged his tail.

Lucky dog, I thought. He didn't have *anything* to worry about.

By the time we got back into the kitchen, the table was set. And when I say *set*, I mean, set with two complete and separate dinners.

The left side of the table was clearly Granny M's dinner: turkey, cranberry sauce, mashed potatoes, spiced apples, homemade bread, sweet potato soufflé, and green bean casserole. On the right side was Peking duck with plum sauce and handmade wrappers, egg rolls, a whole steamed fish, and a stir-fry of mixed vegetables. That was Wai Po's.

Maybe this was going to be my last Thanksgiving dinner ever. Or anybody's last Thanksgiving dinner. If it was in fact my last Thanksgiving, I supposed I wouldn't want it any other way. I just hoped that they would get along, just this once, so I could have a happy memory.

Mr. Pickens smiled as he sat down and rubbed his hands together. "Well, look at that. It's an East-meets-West Thanksgiving. I am a very fortunate man."

Mr. Pickens just might be the key to my hopes for a peaceful Thanksgiving. It didn't hurt that my mom seated him right between Wai Po and Granny M. He could be a buffer.

Mom sat down at the table last, even though it didn't look like she got to cook anything on her menu. She took off her apron and pulled back her hair. "Why don't you say the blessing over the Thanksgiving dinner, David," she said.

Granny M didn't miss a beat. "In Hebrew."

"The turkey isn't even kosher," I said.

"It's still good practice," said my grandmother. She turned to Mr. Pickens. "David is having his bar mitzvah in January, so he needs to practice."

"How wonderful," said Mr. Pickens. "Knowing a second language is so important." Granny M beamed in agreement.

What I really wanted to say was, *Please, God, don't let the Soviets or my grandmothers blow us up on Thanksgiving Day.* But I didn't know how to say that in Hebrew. The only specific food blessings I could say were for bread and wine. And then there's the one that ends *"shehakol nihiyah bed'varo,"* which is supposed to cover a lot of the other stuff. We said it over candy at Hebrew school, so I figured that one would work. I also threw in *tzipur,* which is the Hebrew word for "bird" since we had two of them, the duck and the turkey.

"Gross," said Lauren, who also knew the Hebrew word for bird. "I don't want to think of it as a *bird.* I want to think of it as *dinner.*" She was wearing a button with a picture of Boy George, who was the lead singer for Culture Club. I thought she should have one for a band with a Thanksgiving theme, like the Eagles or America, but she didn't like them.

"The Chinese word for Thanksgiving is *gan en jie,*" said Wai Po.

I guessed I'd better say something in Chinese, too. *"Wo*

xihuan gan en jie," I said. *I like Thanksgiving.* I was relieved to see Wai Po smile. So far, so good.

"I think we should all go around the table and say what we're thankful for," my mother said. This was one of her favorite traditions, even though it was awkward, year after year. "I am thankful that we can all be here, together, as a family. And that we can all remember how lucky we are."

My dad went next. "I am thankful I don't have to work until tonight so I can be here with all of you," he said. My mother smiled. "And I'm thankful that the game is on TV." My mother glared. His mother glared, too. "I am thankful for healthy children and that we have food on our table, and that today, at least, the world is at peace." My mother smiled again, but Granny M cleared her throat, as though she was waiting for something. "I'm glad my mother is closer to us—physically. And I hope she knows she's always been close in our hearts."

My grandmother smiled. My dad had really figured her out over the years, which was a good thing. Then it was her turn.

"I'm thankful to be near my precious grandchildren, even though I am not in the bosom of the family and even if there's no Waldbaum's and I can't find a decent bagel."

I peeked over at Wai Po, and I swear she was smiling when Granny M said that.

"You're around the corner," my father said, and I thought maybe he *hadn't* learned, because this was definitely the time to be quiet.

"That's not the bosom," Granny M said. "That's an arm. Or an elbow." She smiled like she was kidding, but she was showing too many teeth to be kidding.

Mr. Pickens coughed. Hearing Granny M talk about *bosoms* multiple times was probably as embarrassing for him as it was for me.

She changed the subject. Almost. "I'm glad we are all alive, when so many enemies have sought to destroy us." That was a line from the Haggadah, which we read on Passover. "And I'm thankful my family survived the Holocaust."

Mr. Pickens made these sympathetic clicking noises that old people make.

"I didn't think any of our relatives were in the Holocaust," Lauren said.

"Not direct relatives," said Granny M. "Not my sister or my parents, thank God. But relatives. Aren't I allowed to be thankful that they survived? And of course, I am thankful for my grandchildren, who are growing and blossoming before my very eyes. Or, at least, around the corner from my very eyes."

Mr. Pickens said he was grateful to be spending Thanksgiving with neighbors. "And for all of this delicious food," he said. "Without you, I would have only been grateful for a TV dinner."

Wai Po nodded. Then she said: "I am thankful for Bao Bao. And all of you. I am thankful also for the survival of my own family, through difficult times, when we survived the Japanese occupation, when we fled the Communists and went to Taiwan. When I was a girl . . ." And she launched into a history lesson on China that started with the invention of paper and went through the Cultural Revolution.

Granny M looked at the ceiling and muttered, "My people know about difficult times, believe me."

Wai Po stopped talking and looked at her as if Mr. Pickens's head wasn't even there. She gave the most forced smile in the history of the world. Granny M force-smiled back, right through Mr. Pickens. Technically, though, they were still getting along.

Before Wai Po could start talking again, Mom nudged Lauren to take her turn.

"I'm thankful there's no school today and tomorrow," she said. "I'm thankful for my family and my friends. And I'd be really thankful if someone bought me a—"

"This is not the time to talk about Hanukkah presents," my mother said.

"I'm thankful for music," Lauren said.

My mother smiled again and Granny M said, "So talented, my granddaughter."

Mr. Pickens leaned forward and looked at Lauren's button. "Is that a man wearing makeup? What strange times we live in."

Lauren shrugged. "He's a very good singer," she said. "And it's the song that's important, not what he looks like."

I had to admire Lauren for sticking up for Boy George.

Mom looked at me. "It's your turn, David."

"I already went," I reminded her. "I said the first prayer."

"But you didn't say what you were thankful for."

I thought about the things I was truly thankful for: I was thankful that Kelli Ann smelled like apple blossoms and that I wasn't the slowest kid in my PE class and that I grew two inches over the summer and that my mom still put Little Debbie Snack Cakes in my lunch box even though I was in junior high. I was thankful we had won the school-wide trivia contest. I was thankful that my grandmothers hadn't killed each other yet. I was thankful that the world hadn't blown up, although things weren't looking good, so maybe I should really be thankful for the shelter Scott and I were building.

"I'm thankful for everyone here," I said out loud. And then my eyes watered because I really *was* thankful for everyone.

"Is that all?" my mother said.

I tried not to think about the Soviets and missiles, but trying *not* to think of something was pretty much a guaranteed way to think of something. I nodded.

Finally, we were able to eat. You'd think that part

would have been fine, since people were chewing.

Mr. Pickens probably thought Wai Po and Granny M were being polite, because to an untrained ear, they did sound as if they were being nice to each other. But I could hear what they were really saying.

Wai Po took a bite of Granny M's mashed potatoes. "It's very smooth," she said. "You don't even need teeth to eat this." Translation: *These potatoes have no texture. It's like eating baby food.*

"I'm actually one of those odd fellows that likes a lump or two in my potatoes," said Mr. Pickens. "Makes me feel like it's really homemade."

Nobody laughed and I guess Mr. Pickens noticed, because he took a huge serving of turkey to make up for the fact that he wanted lumpy potatoes.

"Would you please pass the spiced apples?" asked Granny M. "I've loved them since I was a little girl." Translation: *I am not eating any Chinese food because it's not traditional.*

Mr. Pickens passed the apples. "Of course." Translation: *I have no idea I'm in the middle of the great Thanksgiving Table War of 1983.*

Wai Po served Mr. Pickens some Peking duck. "Look at that," said Mr. Pickens. "Nice and juicy." He poked the duck with his fork.

"You are very kind," said Wai Po. Translation: *My food is getting compliments!*

"Yes, I can't believe how juicy that duck is, after it was hung up in the garage all day," said Granny M. Translation: *Food should not be hung up in a garage. It should be kept in a refrigerator.* "Here, have some of my green bean casserole. It's not Thanksgiving without my version." She heaped a dollop of casserole on his plate, covering up most of the duck.

Mr. Pickens took a bite of the duck, followed quickly by the green beans. "They're both delicious," he announced. He glanced around the table and said, "I guess it's a good thing my mother taught me to clean my plate." He laughed, though I thought he sounded a little nervous.

"I'm going to give you the best part of this fish," said Wai Po, adding a piece to Mr. Pickens's plate. "No bones."

"This bread is homemade," said Granny M, sawing off a large slice. "I only make it for special occasions."

Mr. Pickens worked his way through a slice of turkey, a slice of duck, a heap of green bean casserole, the bread, and the piece of fish. Just as his plate was almost empty, though, Wai Po added some stir-fried vegetables.

"For digestion," she said. "Chinese vegetables are very good."

"Apples are the best for digestion," said Granny M, also putting some apples on Mr. Pickens's plate.

Under the rules of good Chinese hosting, Wai Po was, technically, doing the right thing by not letting Mr. Pickens have an empty plate. I suspected, though, that she also wanted to show off as many dishes as she could. At the same time, Granny M was not going to let Mr. Pickens eat more Chinese food than her food. Mr. Pickens was trying to keep them both happy by eating all the food they piled on his plate, but he *was never going to finish.*

He picked up a forkful of apples like a condemned man.

"Did you have gravy with your turkey?" asked Granny M. "I don't like to brag, but the cousin of a food magnate once said my gravy should be world famous." She picked up the silver gravy boat and passed it to Mr. Pickens.

"The gravy is very important," said Wai Po. "Since the turkey is so dry."

Mom made a strangled noise and said something in Chinese.

"It's a compliment!" insisted Wai Po. "I think Americans like their meat very dry, right?"

Mr. Pickens opened his mouth and closed it. There was no good way to answer this question. I jumped in.

"I like the turkey," I said. I cut a generous bite of turkey and stuffed it in my mouth, and swallowed. Or tried to swallow. But something wasn't right. Something wasn't right at all.

I looked around the table but everyone was still being perfectly normal. Except me. I couldn't breathe.

I waved my arms like a duck *and* a turkey. No one looked in my direction. I couldn't make the meat go down. I couldn't make it come back up. Mom was talking to Wai Po, and Dad, Lauren, and Granny M were passing bowls of food around. Mr. Pickens was looking down at his plate. I felt like I was trapped under glass. My whole body sent out one message: AIR AIR AIR.

Was this going to be it for me? I'd avoid nuclear war because I choked to death on Thanksgiving dinner? I imagined the headline: DEAD TURKEY KILLS LOCAL BOY. What about my bar mitzvah? Kelli Ann? Who would Scott invite into the shelter to take my place?

Lauren gave me a funny look. Then she said: "Is David . . ."

Suddenly, I remembered something from health class last year. *Save yourself.* I gripped the edge of the table, and forced myself to stand up. I managed to make a tiny noise. *Muh-muh-muh.*

"He's choking!" Mom yelled.

I felt like I was going to pass out. I spun the dining chair around, and rammed my gut onto the back of the chair to give myself the Heimlich maneuver. Instead, I jabbed myself in the ribs. I was about to do it again, but my dad grabbed me around the waist and positioned his fist above my belly-button. He made a motion that was more of a squeeze than a punch. Something shot out of my mouth and bounced across the table. A cool rush of air filled my body. I never thought that breathing could feel like drinking, but those breaths felt like cold water after running a mile on a hot day.

Dad helped me sit down again. "Are you okay?" He stared into my eyes and grabbed my wrist for a pulse. My eyes were watering again, but I wasn't crying.

"Is he going to be okay?" yelled Mom. She had somehow moved to the phone in the kitchen and I could hear a clear, nasally voice come over the other end. "Nine-one-one. What is your emergency?"

Mom waited for the all-clear signal from Dad, and then told the dispatcher that she thought I'd be okay, that I was choking but that the food had been "dislodged" and we had a registered nurse in the house who could vouch for me, and that she was sorry for disturbing them on a holiday. I took a gulp from a glass of water.

Mom walked back into the dining room. After giving me a hug and saying, "Oh, David," she flopped into her chair.

Dad patted me on the back, like he used to when he was trying to get me to fall asleep. "Smaller bites, okay, David?" At times like this, I was glad Dad was a nurse, even if he didn't pick up on the fact that I was choking right away. He knew how to make me feel like I was going to be all right.

"I don't think I'm hungry anymore," I said.

"Why don't we take a break and relax, and then have dessert in an hour?" said Mom. She folded her hands together and looked at me. "As if I needed a reminder to just be grateful that you're here, Hon."

For a moment, everyone was quiet, except for Mr. Pickens, who was still trying to catch up with all the food my grandmothers had heaped on his plate. I thought, *This is probably what other people's Thanksgivings felt like: being grateful for everyday things.* Like breathing. And feeling peaceful and surrounded by people you loved, including two crazy grandmothers.

It's all going to be okay, I thought. As long as we're together and remember what's important in life. All we needed was a little reminder to take care of one another.

Then Wai Po said, "Don't feel bad, Marjorie, that David choked on your dry meat. It is a wonder everybody is not choking to death."

"Do I look as though I feel bad?" said Granny M. "I'm more concerned about that duck, being made in the garage of all places. But don't worry about that now. Thank goodness my Ben saved him."

Their words sounded like they should be nice, *don't feel bad, don't worry,* but they weren't. They were fighting without fighting, which was worse than open hostility in my book. Instead of focusing on the miracle of life and the importance of making the most of these uncertain times, they were using my near-death experience to bicker.

"Let's just be grateful that everything is okay," said Dad. He turned to Mr. Pickens. "Don, shall we go check the scores on TV?"

Mr. Pickens looked green. "I think I may have to head home," said Mr. Pickens, even though he had not cleaned his plate. "I promised my son I'd give him a call. Thanks so much, Ben. Natalie." He smiled at my parents and looked around for his jacket.

"But you haven't had dessert yet!" protested Granny M.

"We both made desserts," said Wai Po.

"You could have coffee," said Granny M.

"Or tea," added Wai Po.

"May I have my jacket?" Mr. Pickens pleaded with my dad.

"Don't go yet," said Granny M.

"Stay longer," ordered Wai Po. It was the first thing they'd agreed on all day.

"I think I need some fresh air," I told Mom. She looked skeptical, so I added, "I'll take Bao Bao out." I whistled for him.

"Oh, I need to let out my dog, too!" said Mr. Pickens, inching toward the door. "Poor Rocky. I don't like to leave him for very long."

Both grandmothers reluctantly agreed that this was a good reason to let Mr. Pickens leave.

"Let me wrap you up some dessert, at least," my mother said. "You can take it with you."

My grandmothers practically ran to the kitchen to get equal servings of dessert wrapped in aluminum foil. They packed up some extra turkey for Rocky, too. Mr. Pickens clutched his packets and flew out the door.

I decided not to tell anyone that Mr. Pickens's dog died last year.

Mom made Lauren go with me and Bao Bao, "just in case," which was fine. I'm not sure what she was worried about, since everyone had witnessed that the piece of turkey was no longer stuck in my throat. It's not like I was going to have a relapse. Lauren pulled on her headphones and began singing along to Kajagoogoo, a band she didn't even have a button for yet. Her singing was actually pretty good, but I motioned for her to take off her headphones.

She pressed the stop button with a hard click. "What?"

"What do you mean what? The dinner? The disaster?"

"I thought they were going to get into a fistfight," she said.

"Well, there's always dessert," I mumbled. "Look, we have to figure this out. What if they mess up my bar mitzvah? And if they mess up mine, they'll probably mess up yours."

"Maybe I'll just take a trip," said Lauren calmly. "I could go to Israel."

I wish I had thought of that.

I grabbed a few pinecones and tossed them into a white plastic bag. Bao Bao inspected a fire hydrant.

"What are you doing?" Lauren wanted to know.

"Something Wai Po does," I said. I started to explain. I swung the bag around like a helicopter blade. It made a whipping noise as it sliced through the air.

Then my bag hit something and I had even more explaining to do.

Here's another question for the How to Talk to Girls

category of Trivial Pursuit. Say you just whacked Kelli Ann Majors in the face with what's supposed to be a bag of poop. Do you:

Continue to pretend that the bag is full of dog poop, and thereby forever create, in her mind, a link between you and dog poop?

OR

Cop to only pretending to pick up dog poop, and thereby forever create, in her mind, a link between you and *fake* dog poop? And lying.

I ended up doing something else altogether, which was trip over Bao Bao's leash and fall to the ground while saying something suave, like *Garoooaggaaa*.

Lauren and Kelli Ann leaned over me. Bao Bao wrapped the leash around me one more time and began licking my face. Considering the last thing I saw him doing with that tongue, I was not too excited about this.

"Are you okay, David?" said Kelli Ann. "I didn't mean to freak you out." She adjusted her hat. It was green, which made her dark eyes more noticeable.

"He's fine," said Lauren, less sympathetically. She grabbed my hand, pulling me to my feet. "You're so weird."

"The button girl!" Kelli Ann said.

"That's Lauren," I said.

Kelli Ann pointed to my bag. "I don't want to ask. But is that dog . . ."

I quickly decided—fake dog poop was still better than dog poop. "Poop?" I held up the bag and let out a big laugh, like the last thing a person would have in a bag while walking a dog was *poop*. "No, no. It's pinecones."

"Pinecones?" Kelli Ann shook her head. "Why are you carrying pinecones in a plastic bag?"

Why indeed? I looked at Lauren, who gave me the you're-on-your-own look.

"Why am I carrying pinecones in a plastic bag?" I said, stalling for time.

"Ye-esss." From the tone of her voice, Kelli Ann was no longer worried about my physical well-being. It was my mental state that was now in question.

I looked at the Masons' house; it was across the street from Grandma's house, and they'd already started decorating for Christmas, which is something people around here do on Thanksgiving Day, don't ask me why.

"For a wreath," I said. "A pinecone wreath."

"A wreath?"

"Yes."

"'Cause we're *Jewish*," said Lauren, not-so-helpfully. I gave her the evil eye behind Kelli Ann's back.

"Hanukkah wreath," I mumbled. I'd never even seen a Hanukkah wreath, probably because they didn't exist. But it sounded like something that could exist. The Abrams put up blue and yellow Christmas lights and called them "Hanukkah lights."

"Wait," said Kelli. "I thought you were Chinese?"

"I'm both," I told her. "You can be Chinese and Buddhist, or Chinese and Taoist, or Chinese and Jewish." I managed to stop blathering before I paired being Chinese with every religion on earth.

"But there aren't too many Chinese Jews around here," I added. It almost felt like a trivia question. *How many Chinese Jews live in Virginia?* Answer: *Ha-ha-ha—what are you talking about?*

Kelli Ann knelt on the ground and stroked Bao Bao. He was sniffing around, the way he did right before he dropped a load. *Please don't poop, please don't poop in front of Kelli Ann,* I thought. Wonder of wonders, Bao Bao seemed to hear me. He stopped sniffing and wagged his tail. "He's cute," Kelli Ann said. She looked up at me. "You don't look—"

I thought she was going to say *Jewish*. A lot of people say that. Even my great-aunt Seal said that when I was born, which is one of the reasons my grandmother doesn't speak to her. But what Kelli Ann said was, "like a crafty person."

Did she mean crafty like a person who does crafts, or crafty, like sneaky? The truth was, I wasn't either.

"So how do you make a Hanukkah wreath?" Kelli Ann asked.

"Well, uh, you put dreidels and gelt on it," I said. "And, uh, a menorah and Star of David." I went through every Hanukkah icon that existed, except potato latkes. Then I waited for lightning to strike. The wind blew a little, but the sky stayed clear.

"And pinecones," Lauren added.

"Is that a Jewish tradition?" said Kelli Ann. "I've never seen a Hanukkah wreath before."

"It's not a tradition," I said. "It's new."

"Totally," Lauren said. "You should come over and see it when David's done." I waited until Kelli Ann looked at Bao Bao again before I mouthed *I'm going to get you* at Lauren and made the international sign for strangling.

"If it's this weekend, I can't. Gotta do the divorced parent rotation, you know." Kelli Ann twirled her finger in her hair. "I have to eat *two* complete Thanksgiving dinners. My dad's

girlfriend's parents live over here. Well, over there, actually."
She pointed behind her. "I should probably be heading back.
I said I was just coming out for some fresh air."

"Hey, me too," I said.

"You're missing out," Lauren said. "David's Hanukkah
wreaths are *the best*."

"The best," I agreed.

"I'll probably be back over before Christmas—I mean,
winter break," said Kelli Ann. She turned and did a fluttery
thing with her fingers. "Bye."

*Say something, you idiot. Tell her she's amazing. Tell her
you'll save her a spot in the bomb shelter.*

Uh.

"Yee lou sater," I said.

Kelli Ann turned back around and wrinkled her nose at
me. "What?"

"See you back at school," I said.

I watched her walk away. "You like her," Lauren said,
nudging me.

"Shut up."

"I think she likes you."

I couldn't help myself. "You do?"

"I'm pretty sure," said Lauren. "Did you notice how she
started to say *Christmas break,* and then switched to *winter
break*? She's trying to be considerate."

I thought this over. The signs of someone liking you
were pretty hard to spot.

"It's really too bad," said Lauren.

"Why? Why is it too bad?"

Lauren curled Bao Bao's leash in her hand. "'Cause Granny M's going to kill you when she finds out you're making a Hanukkah wreath."

I made a Hanukkah wreath anyway, in case Kelli Ann

decided to come over. It wasn't attractive, but it definitely said Hanukkah. I spray-painted the pinecones blue and yellow. I found some plastic dreidels in a box in the basement. I also cut out Stars of David from aluminum foil. I bought some gelt and glued that on, too.

Granny M didn't kill me when she saw it. But she sighed enough to blow over a small shed. Then she made a request.

"I want you to start calling me *safta*," she said. "It means 'grandmother' in Hebrew."

"What's wrong with Granny M?" I asked.

"*Safta* is more Jewish."

"I thought *bubbe* was more Jewish," I said.

"My sister, Seal, uses *bubbe*," she said. "You know what my nephew called her when he was little? *Booby*. No, I think I make a better *safta*. Using Jewish words will help you get in the spirit of things. You're not in touch with your Jewish roots."

Wai Po wasn't going to let *that* fly by. "I think you should also be spending some time learning Chinese. We can speak it together," she said. "*Ni jiao shenma mingzi?*"

I knew a little Chinese, but it was pretty rusty. I took a chance. "I'm twelve," I said.

Wai Po narrowed her eyes. "I just asked you what your name was."

Mud, I thought. *My name is mud.* I called Scott and asked him if we could work on the hole.

When I got to the hole, Scott had a whole setup: soda, candy, and Funyuns. Most impressively, though, he had brought a boom box so we could listen to the radio.

"No reason why preparing for the end of the world can't be a little fun," said Scott. He turned on the radio and fiddled with the antenna.

"Nice," I said.

"It'd be better if it was a TV, with *Battlestar Galactica*," said Scott.

"No way! *Star Trek* is way better."

Hector and I had never debated the relative merits of *Star Trek* versus *Battlestar Galactica* because Hector did not like science fiction. He hadn't even seen *Star Wars*. Once I told him I wanted a light saber for my birthday, and he wanted to know if he could get one at Sears.

Scott was ready to argue, though.

"Nah. *Star Trek*'s all, everybody gets along on the

Enterprise, tra-la-la, and we have to teach people on other planets to be like us," he said. "That's garbage. As long as there are people, there are problems, you know?"

The radio was playing "Let's Dance" when the music was interrupted by an annoying whine. It was the Emergency Broadcast System, testing to make sure all the radio and TV frequencies were working. It came with an announcement that everyone could recite from memory because it seemed to come on all the time. The high-pitched tone was only supposed to last about thirty seconds, but it always seemed longer.

I was going to reach over and turn off the radio, but Scott stopped me. "You need to listen to it now. If there's an attack, this is one way we'll find out."

My heart sped up. I'd never thought about that—only how irritating it was to wait. At the end, when they said it was just a test, I realized I'd been holding my breath. The announcement ended, *If this had been an actual emergency, the Attention Signal you just heard would have been followed by official information, news, or instructions.*

Scott chuckled and said, "One down, about a million to go."

"I can't imagine them saying anything except it was just a test. What are they going to say, *this is real and you're probably going to die?*"

"Maybe."

"I'm not sure I'd want to know."

"Forewarned is forearmed," said Scott. "Let's just keep digging."

The Emergency Broadcast System had put a damper on our mood, even though the radio station started playing music again, as if nothing had happened. Scott opened the bag of Funyuns, pulled out a few rings, and then handed the bag to me.

"Okay," said Scott. "Think about this. Things You Need and Can Take. Things You Need and Cannot Take."

"Huh? Take where?"

Scott pointed at the hole. "The shelter. Gotta think ahead."

"Oh, okay. We need food and can take food. Nonperishables, like tuna and peanut butter."

"How about Chun King?"

"Chinese food from a can will not help anyone survive," I said. I wondered what food would help us the most. "We might need more water than we can take."

"Excellent point," said Scott. "We'll have to figure out how to ration out water, because we'll die of thirst before we'll die of starvation."

"Right," I said.

"Now, Things You Want and Can Take."

"I'd want to take books."

"Yeah, books and magazines. Have you read Douglas Adams?"

"Everyone has," I said. Except Hector, of course.

"I have a set," said Scott. "I'll bring them. Do you play chess?"

"I know how the pieces move, but I haven't played that many games."

"I'll bring a chess set, too. Chess is the best game, because it doesn't depend on luck. Also, it takes a long time to play." Scott pushed the shovel into the ground with his foot. The hole was slowly getting deeper, but it still needed to be widened. "We're going to have a lot of time to kill."

"I'll bring cards," I said. *Hector would hate this,* I thought. Talking about science fiction and chess. Hector hated board games, too, except for Trivial Pursuit. When we were little, he hated Candy Land because he didn't want to be the winner or the loser.

Scott handed me the shovel. "Okay, last one. Things You Want and Cannot Take."

The first thing I thought of was Hector and Kelli Ann and my family. But that wasn't what Scott meant.

"What's on your list?" I asked.

"Television and my Atari," said Scott. "A real bed."

"Juice, going to the movies, and . . ." I thought about it. "School?"

"School?" Scott kicked at the pile of dirt next to the hole. "You'd miss school?"

"Well, not homework and tests. The fun part, like seeing friends." *Like Hector,* I added silently.

"If you mean friends, then say friends," said Scott. "No one says what they mean anymore. My parents, they're the worst."

I thought about my family, being together at Thanksgiving. It wasn't a Norman Rockwell portrait of a family gathering, but it was us.

"I'd miss my family," I said.

Scott shook his head. "Not me. And you shouldn't, either."

"You said to say what I mean."

Scott took the shovel to scrape some dirt off his shoe. "You can't think of those things. Don't think of things you can't have, even after you survive. I can have a soft bed again, or food that doesn't come in a can. Don't go for, whaddaya-callit, intangibles."

"I think you mean people," I said.

"I'm talking about things that can't be replaced," said Scott. "Focus on juice."

"Maybe we won't have trees," I said. "After."

"We can bring some seeds," said Scott. "In fact, we should bring different kinds of fruit seeds, just in case we need to plant trees. Apples, peaches. Maybe bananas if the climate changes."

I had to give it to Scott. That was a good idea, even if I

wasn't sure what banana seeds looked like. I jumped down into the hole. Only my head and shoulders were above ground. It was almost deep enough to make one of us safe. "It's looking pretty good, huh?"

"Yeah," said Scott. "We should start expanding soon. Then we can get a cover to put over the top."

Soon? If we couldn't even stand up straight, things were going to be pretty cramped. "Doesn't it need to be deeper?" I said. "Especially for you, since you're taller?"

"Why? You want to dig to China?"

That saying's always bugged me. Why China, especially since, if we dug straight through from where we were standing, we'd actually end up in the Pacific Ocean? And then I wondered: What do kids in China say when they're digging a big hole?

"We have to hurry," said Scott. "You want to get fried just because you wanted roomier quarters?"

The problem with planning for a nuclear war was that you never knew exactly when it could happen. It was any time between never and five minutes from now.

"I'm going to miss standing up," I said.

Scott laughed.

I thought of something. "You know, we *could* bring our families. We could just make the hole wider."

"No," said Scott. "No families."

Sometimes when people say *no*, you can hear a yes in their voice. Maybe it's because they hesitate before they speak, or they fudge their answer with words like *not right now*. But the way Scott said *no*, you could tell that his answer was not about to change.

"Look," said Scott. He was standing at the top of the hole, so he looked twice as tall. "Once you involve families, you start making choices. Like you and your crazy grandmothers. They fight, right?"

"You could say that."

"So what if they're driving everyone crazy, and finally you decide that one of them has to go. How would you choose?"

I reached up and put my hands on the ground, and then used them to pull myself out of the hole. Considering how many pull-ups I usually completed for the Presidential Physical Fitness Test, this was a pretty big accomplishment. "Maybe they'd stop fighting if they knew one of them was going to get kicked out."

"No," said Scott. "They'd keep fighting. They can't help it. You have to choose one."

"Come on," I said.

"No, really. You have to. Choose."

I closed my eyes and tried to choose, but all I could imagine was one of the grandmothers outside the shelter, crying and begging to come back in.

Last year, Mom and Dad saw this really depressing movie called *Sophie's Choice*. It was about this woman who could only save one of her children from the Nazis. How could she choose? How could anyone?

"I can't," I said.

"See?" said Scott. "No families." His tone softened. "It's just the way it's gotta be. It saves a lot of trouble, trust me."

As I was getting ready to leave, Scott reached into his backpack and handed me a book.

It was the fourth Douglas Adams book, *So Long, and Thanks for All the Fish*. No one had this book.

"Whoa—where'd you get this?" I turned the book over in my hands. It wasn't even supposed to come out until next year.

"It's an early copy, for book reviewers and stuff. My dad's friend gave it to him."

"Nice." I tried to hand him the book back.

"Take it. I've already read it." When I didn't say okay right away, Scott said, "Look, it could be just the two of us, if someone pushes the button. What's mine is yours."

I hesitated—it felt as if this was sealing the deal, that I was agreeing not to talk about Hector or families anymore.

I took the book and crossed my fingers.

Because of the Hanukkah wreath, Granny M, I mean

Safta, made what was the equivalent of a 911 call to the rabbi. I didn't actually see her make the call, but at the beginning of our next meeting, Rabbi Doug asked me if I knew what "assimilation" meant.

"This is about the wreath, isn't it?" I said.

He smiled. "Look, I know what it's like to feel left out, David," he said. He pronounced it the Hebrew way, which is more like *Dah-veed.* "I'm just saying we can appreciate someone else's traditions without adopting them for our own."

"I know."

"We don't need a Hanukkah bush or a Dreidel Man in order to fit in."

"I know," I said again.

"We have a long and proud tradition of our own."

"I *know.*"

"If you're ever in doubt, think about the food," he said. "We have them beat on the food. I'd take rugelach over a fruit cake any day. Or babka. Babka beats fruitcake."

But what about Chinese Jews? I wanted to ask him. *What is their long and proud tradition?* I didn't ask, though, because I was pretty sure he wouldn't know.

He winked and turned back to the Torah. Rabbi Doug was still trying to teach me the trope, which is the melody you use when you're chanting your haftorah or Torah portion. I always thought it was random, but there were actually little marks to tell you when your voice goes up and when it goes down. Usually, I went down when I should be going up, even though the rabbi put the whole thing on a cassette tape so I could practice at home.

"Closer," said Rabbi Doug. I couldn't tell if I was really getting closer or if he was just saying that. I didn't think rabbis were supposed to lie, though. "Do you mind if I take off my shoes?" he said.

"No, it's okay. We do it at my house all the time," I said, because who is going to tell a rabbi he can't take his shoes off in his own office? Besides, maybe it would make him think I was doing a better job, if he was comfortable.

"Again," he said.

My reading was going pretty badly when there was a knock on the door of the study. The rabbi padded over to the door in his socks. I didn't mind the interruption, until I saw who it was.

"Granny M?"

"Hello, Rabbi," said Grandma Marjorie. "We spoke on the phone earlier. David's *safta*?" Argh, I'd forgotten to use *safta* again. "I would never interrupt, but this is important—I want to talk about David's bar mitzvah. Something I saw when I was in New York."

"They do things differently in New York," said Rabbi Doug. He gave me a smile that said he liked the way we did things here a little better. And he winked again. "Besides, I don't have anything to do with the reception."

"This isn't about the reception," Safta said. "Why should I trouble a rabbi about the reception? This is about the service. It's about finding David's Russian twin."

My spine went cold. I had a Russian twin? Was there someone who looked just like me in Russia? Maybe we all had twins in Russia as part of some bizarre genetic program.

"I've heard about this," said Rabbi Doug.

"I haven't," I said. "I haven't heard *anything* about this."

"The rabbi can explain," Safta said.

Rabbi Doug nodded again. "In Russia, children are not free to celebrate a bar or bat mitzvah, so in some countries where the children *are* free, they may decide to celebrate for a 'twin' back in the Soviet Union." He looked at my grandmother. "Did you attend a bar mitzvah like this?"

"It was Jacob's bar mitzvah," said my grandmother. "My sister, Seal's, grandson. He had a Russian twin."

Ah, that explained it. My great-aunt Seal. Again.

"I don't have an actual twin?" I said.

"What?" said my grandmother. "What are you talking about?"

"A twi—" the rabbi began. "No. A 'Russian twin' is someone whose birthday is near the birthday of the bar mitzvah boy. You're bonded by birthdays, not blood. And you're bound by a spirit of helping another human being. I've heard about synagogues doing this but we haven't tried it here. You could be the first. Sharing your bar mitzvah with someone who can't have one? I could get behind a trend like that."

"To top it off, Seal's grandson gave half his bar mitzvah money to his twin," my grandmother continued. "To help him emigrate to Israel. He's a mensch, my nephew. Not that Seal had anything to do with it."

Not that she'd know, since they still weren't talking. This made me not want to talk to my grandmother, either. Giving away half my money to someone I'd never even met? What kind of idea was that? You'd think that with money so tight because of the bar mitzvah my parents would at least want me to keep it for college, instead of giving it away to a stranger.

"It sounds wonderful," Rabbi Doug said. "Do you know the organization that does the matches?"

I hoped my grandmother hadn't gone too far into her research, but she reached into her purse and pulled out a folded slip of paper. She waved it at the rabbi.

"If you approve, we will take care of it," Safta said. "I'll wait outside."

"Maybe you'd like your grandmother to stay and listen," Rabbi Doug said to me. His eyes twinkled. "After all, it looks like you're learning for two now." He made it sound like I was pregnant.

"No," I said. My grandmother looked a little offended, so I added, "I want it to be a surprise." Rabbi Doug smiled and changed the subject.

"I know some Russian," said Rabbi Doug. "*Spasibo* means 'thank you.'"

I imagined my Russian twin saying *spasibo* for half of the bar mitzvah money.

"I'll just wait in the front hall until your lesson is over," my grandmother told me. To the rabbi, she said, "Let me know if I can do anything else to help."

You've already done enough, I thought. I wondered how to say *mind your own business* in Russian. Or Hebrew. But the only language I knew it in was English, and I didn't have the guts to say it out loud.

15

Of course Rabbi Doug was a big fan of my grandmother's idea. So were my parents.

"This is what it's all about," my dad said.

"I thought that was the hokey pokey," I said. I put my right foot out in case nobody got my joke, but either they didn't hear me or they didn't laugh.

"We should put a little note in the invitation about the Russian twin," said Mom. "Maybe we can get a picture of him."

"You're not putting in a picture of David," Lauren pointed out, which was what I had been thinking. Lauren was so lucky. She wasn't going to get any weird surprises for her bat mitzvah; she'd be *prepared* because I was going first, like the first wave of soldiers into battle. I hoped that she might say something about the money, since she would definitely get the same treatment, but she didn't.

"I do not know about this Russian twin," Wai Po said. At least she was on my side. Then she said: "Why doesn't he have a twin who is Chinese?"

"Because a twin from China wouldn't be Jewish," said Safta. "A twin from China wouldn't want a bar mitzvah."

"Do these Russians know that David is Chinese? The Russians and Chinese, they do not always get along," said Wai Po.

"They're both Communist countries," I pointed out.

Wai Po shook her head. "There's a longer history than that."

It's not like the Russians and Americans are best friends, either, I thought, just as Safta said: "David is American and any boy would be grateful to have him as a twin. This is an official program. Seal's grandson did it."

"Seal?" asked Wai Po. "The one who says David doesn't look Jewish? But he's having a bar mitzvah. I think David should think about helping the Chinese. He is Chinese, too, after all." She paused a minute, then added, "Even if he doesn't look totally Chinese."

This had been going on since I was born: Each side of my family thought I looked like I belonged to the other. But when I looked in the mirror, all I saw was me.

Then my mother said the words of doom:

It is up to David to decide who he wants to help.

"Um," I said.

"But we have to decide quickly," said Safta.

"That's true," my mother said. She looked at me. "I do think it would be a lovely thing to do."

Safta nodded. Wai Po looked away.

I'd already lost half of my bar mitzvah money, which I hadn't even gotten yet, and now Wai Po wanted the other half. Sure, I was probably better off than kids in either of those countries, but that didn't mean I didn't want my bar mitzvah money, even if I was supposed to put most of it in a savings account.

My father said, "A bar mitzvah is a celebration of the Jewish part of David's life." It was like he was leading me right to the answer instead of making me decide. It didn't feel like I had much of a choice anyway.

"I guess I could share my bar mitzvah with a Russian twin," I said finally. "But do you think he could be the only one?" I thought about Lauren's button, the one that said, EXPERIENCE IS WHAT YOU GET WHEN YOU DON'T GET WHAT YOU WANT. I was getting a lot of experience.

Wai Po squeezed her lips together and I was afraid she was mad that I didn't want a twin from China, too. Then she gave me a little smile and I realized: She didn't need me to have a twin back in China. She just wanted to get under Granny M's skin.

"Well, I think *Da-Wei*," she began, saying my Chinese name extra loud. "I think *Da-Wei* should have his Chinese side represented at the bar mitzvah, too." She folded her arms. "I think there should be Chinese food at the bar mitzvah."

It was going to be Thanksgiving all over again, only this time with a bigger audience. Maybe we should add a note to the invitation. *Please come very hungry. Starving, really.* Also, it would help if we invited a lot of people who knew the Heimlich maneuver.

Safta turned to my parents. "Are you going to allow this?" she asked.

"I don't see why not," said Dad. "It's a nice idea."

Mom put her hands over her eyes, but I knew what she was doing. She was thinking about the money, adding up the dollars in her head. More food = more money.

If I said no to Chinese food, I would hurt Wai Po's feelings, and if I agreed to it, my parents would think I didn't care about the money. So I said nothing.

"No pork," Granny M—Safta—warned Wai Po. "Or shellfish." Even though we didn't keep kosher at home, I had to agree, a pork-fried bar mitzvah did not seem the way to go.

Wai Po turned her chin up. "I know the owner at Bamboo Palace. We can work out something. Chinese food can accommodate many tastes."

Everyone but Safta's, I thought.

I went to my room to finish my math homework before they could figure out more ways to ruin my bar mitzvah. I put my Hebrew tape on in the background, and hoped some of it would sink in.

The next day, while I was at school, my father called the same organization that helped my cousin Jacob find a twin.

"It's a boy!" he announced at dinner. "His name is Alexi. And he's just three weeks older than you are."

"I wanted a sister," Lauren said. "Not another brother." She fiddled with the button on her shirt. It said, SOUNDS LIKE A PERSONAL PROBLEM TO ME.

"Thanks a lot," I said.

"You should write him a letter," my mother said, ignoring Lauren. "Introduce yourself. Explain what we're doing. Get to know each other."

Wasn't it enough that this kid was getting half my money? "Why?" I said.

"Because it will be more meaningful if you have a real connection," my mother said.

"It's like homework," I said.

"It's a letter," said Dad.

I stomped back upstairs without even asking if I could watch TV because I knew what the answer would be. I turned on my Hebrew tape and pulled out a pencil and a piece of paper.

Stupid. Stupid. Stupid.

I thought about what to write.

Dear Alexi,

Well, that part was easy enough. The name didn't sound Jewish-Russian, just Russia-Russian, like a spy. I touched the tip of my pencil to my tongue.

In case they haven't told you yet, I'm your new twin brother. I am about to be bar mitzvahed and my parents discovered some international organization so now you are going to be bar mitzvahed, too, through me, I guess. Which sounds weird.

It did sound weird, like I was a vessel or something. It didn't sound very Jewish. But erasing and starting over meant more work, so I kept writing.

I wish you could learn some of the stuff that I'm learning so that I wouldn't have to do it all myself.

I added a "ha" so he would know I was joking, but I kind of wasn't. He could at least do some of the work. My parents had said he *couldn't* do that, given that he wasn't really allowed to practice his religion in Russia and it was already hard enough for him to go to regular school there. Still.

I'm on a trivia team and go to school and practice Hebrew. Also, I am half-Chinese.

I felt like it was important to add the Chinese part. I thought about telling him about the hole we were digging, but that seemed weird, too. *I'm digging a hole in the woods in case your country drops a bomb on mine.* I wondered if they showed *The Day After* in the Soviet Union. I didn't think so. I wasn't even sure they had TV.

I didn't write anything at all for a full five minutes and then I remembered the pen pal trick from when we were writing those kids in Minnesota (the state where both masking and Scotch tape were invented): ask questions.

Do you have electricity? I wrote. *Do you have TV? Do you like sports? What is it like there? What is your favorite food? Do you have a grandmother? Do you have any brothers or sisters? What is your favorite subject in school?*

There. That filled a few more lines.

Sincerely, David

If he wrote back, maybe I'd tell him more about me. But for the moment, that seemed to be all there was to tell. Hopefully my parents wouldn't ask to see the letter before they mailed it. If they did ask, I'd just tell them it was private.

On Thursday at lunch, Hector, Scott, and I practiced

for the tournament. Scott had brought in an old *TV Guide* and we were using it to ask Hector questions. The funny thing about Hector was that he knew that John Wayne's last movie was *The Shootist,* but then he didn't know who Captain Kirk was. "Wouldn't that be a history question or something?" Hector said. "Why is this in the *TV Guide*? What branch of the military was he in?"

Scott had asked Hector this question as a joke, not knowing that Hector didn't like science fiction. Scott turned his head slightly, so Hector couldn't see his expression, and rolled his eyes at me.

"You know," I said. "Captain Kirk. From *Star Trek*?"

"Okay, so you would have gotten that one," said Hector.

"You still need to practice," said Scott. I noticed that he said *you* and not *we.* "You're in charge of all these TV and movie questions. You just got to cram all this stuff in your head."

"Fine. Give me another one." Hector clenched his eyes shut and braced his hands against the lunch table.

"Okay," said Scott. He ran his finger down the page. "*What movie made in 1957 starred Audrey Hepburn and Fred Astaire?*" Right after Scott read the question, Heather Roberts walked up to our table.

"That's not the kind of question they're going to ask," I said. I wasn't sure whether I should say hi or not to Heather. Heather was one of Scott's popular-people friends. She dressed totally preppie. She was wearing two polos with both collars popped.

"If Hector doesn't know it, he doesn't know it," said Scott. Then he turned around. "Heather," said Scott. He leaned back, relaxed. "How's it going?"

"I think I've got this," cried Hector. "It would have to be a musical since Astaire was in it." His eyes were still closed.

Heather looked over at Hector and raised her eyebrows. "Is he okay?"

"He's fine," said Scott. "What's up?"

Heather put her hand on the back of Scott's chair and tilted her head to one side. "I'm mad at you, Scott Dursky. You said you'd let me know what happened in French, remember? I had an ortho appointment." Although Heather *said* she was mad, she sounded anything but.

"It's coming to me!" said Hector. I nudged him so he would shut up. What Scott did was like magic, talking to a girl and being so cool about it. I wanted to hear what he was going to say.

"I'll fill you in later, okay?" said Scott. "I'm busy."

"You'd better," said Heather, and walked away. She never said hi to me or Hector, which was probably a good thing, because about three seconds after she left, Hector screeched, "*FUNNY FACE!*"

Heather spun around. "*Excuse* me?"

"It's a movie," I blurted. "He didn't mean you; you don't have a funny face. You have an average face." Maybe that wasn't the right thing to say. Now Heather's face looked like it belonged in a different kind of movie, one with a body count.

She tossed her head and stalked back to her table.

"*Funny Face* is correct," said Scott.

"But quit shouting," I added. I checked to make sure Kelli Ann wasn't staring at us, along with the rest of the cafeteria.

"Yeah, you're such a weirdo, Hector," said Scott.

Hector took a long sip from his milk carton. "Do you guys want to come over on Friday?" he asked. "We could play some Trivial Pursuit and and my dad rented *First Blood* again. It's rated R, but he says we can watch."

"You mean *Rambo*?" Scott said.

The film starred Sylvester Stallone as a guy who'd served in Vietnam and had PTSD but wasn't fitting back into society because the sheriff in the town he was travelling through was a jerk. There was lots of running and shooting. Also, swearing. Hector's dad had a *thing* about Vietnam, because he actually fought in Vietnam, which was weird because other people I knew who fought in Vietnam didn't want any sort of reminder. Because Hector had that thing for old movies, it was kind of a big deal, wanting to see a movie made in this half of the twentieth century.

"Friday is the first night of Hanukkah, so I can't," I said.

"Well, what about Saturday?"

"I'm busy Saturday afternoon," I said. "But I could go later, maybe." Safta was taking me shopping for a bar mitzvah suit. It was marked on the calendar, with all the appeal of a dentist appointment.

"I'm busy Saturday night," said Scott. "And on Sunday, David and I have a project to work on."

"I could help," offered Hector. "Then you'd be done quicker and we could still do the other stuff."

Scott shook his head before I could say anything. "It's for history. We have Hudson and you have Simmons."

Now I knew Scott was just making up stuff to avoid Hector. We didn't have anything to do for history. And I *wanted* to practice, because it was fun and because we needed to. I was going to say something, maybe not bust Scott, but let Hector know we could work it out, when I saw Heather walk over to Kelli Ann's table, lean down, and whisper. Maybe she was whispering about me.

I had a choice. I could either go hang with Scott, and learn how to talk to girls without mixing up my words or sounding like I was having a panic attack, or I could hang with Hector, and possibly end up being someone who thought that suddenly yelling *funny face* in a crowded cafeteria was a good idea.

It wasn't exactly fair. I apologized to Hector, but in my brain, not out loud. Then I said, "Yeah, Sunday's out. Maybe another time?"

"Don't worry about it," said Hector, way too quickly. He stood up and brushed the crumbs off his shirt, which was one of the ones he'd gotten from Walt Disney World. It had Goofy on it, instead of Mickey, because he felt like Mickey got all of the attention and it wasn't fair to the rest of the characters. "I need to go to the library again. You guys want to come?"

I hadn't finished eating, and Scott just shook his head. As soon as Hector was out of earshot, Scott leaned forward and said, "I've been thinking about it. We're going to have a hard time getting a cover for the shelter. The hole is getting too big, and we need a really thick cover to protect us."

"So what do you want to do about it?" For a second, I got a crazy picture in my head of a long, narrow, deep hole, with us stacked on top of each other.

"We need to make tunnels."

That made more sense. "Tunnels. Like in *The Great Escape*?" *The Great Escape* was an old movie about POWs who secretly dug tunnels to get out of a Nazi prison.

"Exactly. The tunnels will give us room to stretch out, and the earth can provide protection from the radiation."

I thought about it some more. "You remember that in the movie, the tunnels kept collapsing, right?" I felt kind of proud of myself, for thinking of something Scott hadn't considered.

Scott already had an answer. "That dirt was loose. We've got Virginia clay. It's thick. It won't collapse."

I pictured us living in tunnels of dirt like the earthworms the eighth graders thought we were. Maybe we'd meet in the middle and play Trivial Pursuit, to make the time go faster. That made me think of Hector, who wouldn't be there.

"If we make tunnels, we could make room for more people. With tunnels, you don't even really have to hang out with anyone if you don't want to," I said, hoping Scott would get the hint.

"Or just not invite them in the first place," said Scott. "Watch this." He wadded up the wrapper from his hamburger and threw it in an arc. The wad of paper dropped perfectly in the middle of Heather's table of friends. Heather got up and fake-stomped her way back to us.

"Scott Dursky! Quit throwing stuff at our table." You could tell that she was trying to hide a smile.

Scott shrugged. "I was bored."

"You just said that you were *busy* and that's why you couldn't tell me what happened in French."

"I'm not busy anymore," Scott said. "Do you want me to tell you or not?"

Heather smiled. "*Oui*," she said. Heather didn't take notes, but I did, in my head, on how to have an actual conversation with a girl.

When I got home from school on Friday, Safta had

already put Lauren to work, peeling potatoes for latkes. Even though Lauren and I go to the same school, we never walk together and we never arrive at school or home at the same time. I guess it was Lauren's bad luck that she got home first. She looked up long enough to give me a dirty look over the mound of potato peels.

"Did you have a good day at school, David?" asked Safta.

"It was adequate," I told her.

"Well, have a snack and then practice your haftorah," said Safta.

"Whoa, wait a minute," said Lauren. "When I get home, it's *Lauren put your backpack down and help with the potatoes*, and with David, it's *have a snack*?!"

"You can have a snack, too. Have a bite of the potato," said Safta.

"Raw?"

"So have an apple. I'm sorry, princess of my heart, but your brother has to practice."

I actually had no plans to practice my haftorah, but I played along. "I really should get to work." I threw in a sigh for good measure.

Lauren glared at me and then at Safta. She was wearing a yellow smiley face button, but it was the only part of her that seemed happy. "This is so unfair! I bet he's not even going to practice." She put on her headphones and turned on her music, even though Mom has told her that it's rude to listen to music on her Walkman in front of other people.

"Go on and practice, David," said Safta. "We'll take care of this."

Lauren turned away from us to scrape the potato peels into the trash. She had started singing along to the music, telling someone to call her, repeatedly. She sounded just like Deborah Harry, but I wasn't going to tell her that.

After all that, I felt like I had to practice, so I did. I also read a couple of chapters of *So Long, and Thanks for All the Fish*, but no one needed to know that. When I went back downstairs, Lauren wasn't in the kitchen anymore, but Safta was. Bao Bao was trailing after her, half barking, half whining.

"Go away, Boo Boo," Safta said. "I need to fry the latkes." There was a frying pan on the stove, glistening with oil.

"His name is Bao Bao," I reminded her.

Safta tried again. "Bo Bo." This time she made the long *o* sound.

I tried again. "Ow, like when a dog barks. Bowwow. Bao Bao."

"That is not how this animal barks," Safta said. She leaned over and looked Bao Bao directly in the eyes. He sat and wagged his tail. "Go away, dog," she said. "I'm cooking here."

"Is that what you're doing?" Wai Po walked into the kitchen and looked into the pan. "You're doing it wrong."

"I'm doing *what* wrong?" said Safta.

"Cooking."

I thought Safta's head might actually pop off her neck. "Do you mean cooking *latkes*? Is that what you're talking about?"

"If that is what you're making, then yes."

Safta turned and stared at Wai Po. It was hard to tell whether she was smiling or baring her teeth. "I have been making latkes for more years than I can count, and before that, I watched my mother make them, who watched her mother make them, and so on and so on."

"It doesn't matter," said Wai Po. "Doing it wrong for a long time doesn't make it right."

I tried to run interference. "Wai Po, would you like to go for a walk?"

"In a minute."

"I think Bao Bao really has to go."

"He is fine."

Wai Po pulled out her wok and poured oil into it. While it was heating up, she hooked little metal racks to the edge.

"Look," she said. "You put in a whole pancake to see if the oil is hot enough, but all you need is a chopstick. When the chopstick has bubbles, the oil is hot enough. Also, the wok keeps the oil from spattering and making a mess."

"I don't make a mess," said Safta stiffly.

"And you are using paper towels to soak up oil! See, the latkes can just drain on the racks."

Safta sighed. "All of this," she said, waving her hand around in a circle, "is just bells and whistles. Smoke and mirrors. The only thing that really matters with a latke is taste."

"Of course," Wai Po said.

They both set to work, making latkes. Right about the time that the latkes were flipped (Safta used a spatula while Wai Po used chopsticks), I had a really terrible realization.

I was going to be the taste tester.

I started to back out of the kitchen, but they were onto me. Safta held up her hand. "Don't go anywhere, David. We have a job for you."

"Eating my latkes won't be a job," said Wai Po. "It will be a pleasure."

I was trapped. I alone was going to decide which grandmother was going to be happy, and which one was going to be angry, because I was pretty sure they weren't going to accept a tie. Each latke that came out of the pan or wok brought me one step closer to my fate.

But then I thought of something. One person couldn't announce a tie, but *two* people could.

"Lauren!" I shouted. "It's time to eat latkes."

Wai Po leaned over her row of latkes, deciding which one to offer for judging. Safta used her spatula to lift one up to her nose, sniffing it.

The next thing that happened can only be described as a perfect storm, where everything goes wrong. Wai Po turned away from the stove, holding her choice of latke in her chopsticks at the exact same time Safta turned away from the stove, holding *her* choice of latke on the spatula.

The two kitchen utensils clacked together like swords, and sent the spatula latke through the air. It hit Lauren in the face as she walked in the kitchen door.

If you've ever wondered what it sounds like when someone gets hit by a latke, it sounds like a muffled *whap.* If it happens in the presence of two grandmothers, it's a muffled *whap* followed by a pair of shrieks.

"Lauren!" Wai Po dropped her chopsticks and ran. She cradled Lauren's head.

"Let me look!" said Safta.

"Let *me* look," said Dad, who had come to investigate. He turned Lauren's forehead so he could see it properly. "Let's put a cool washcloth on it, just to be on the safe side, but I think she'll be fine."

"This is what happens when there are too many cooks in the kitchen," announced Safta.

"The latke being held by the cook with chopsticks wasn't the one that hit Lauren," responded Wai Po.

Mom came in and dropped her keys on the counter. "What on earth?"

I didn't want to say anything, but at the same time, I didn't want my grandmothers to start in. While I was grasping for the right words, Lauren announced, "I got hit in the face with a latke."

It's very hard to hear the words *I got hit in the face with a latke* without at least smiling a little. Even Safta and Wai Po relaxed.

"Oh, goodness," said Mom.

Lauren moved the washcloth so Mom could see. Even though Dad was the nurse, we always wanted Mom to see our injuries, too. The red mark had faded.

"Looks good," said Mom. "And at least it wasn't David that got it!" She laughed. "We wouldn't want him to have a red mark on his face for his bar mitzvah!"

Lauren looked at me and glared. "It's all about you," she said.

"What do you want me to do about it?" I asked her. "Ask them to throw latkes at my face?"

Stomp. Stomp. Stomp.

Safta and Wai Po went back to work. Between them, we had a whole, giant mountain of latkes in less than forty minutes. We were even more careful than we were at Thanksgiving. Dad, Mom, Lauren, and I all made sure to eat equal numbers of both the traditional and wok-cooked latkes.

Shopping for bar mitzvah clothes with Safta was the

worst possible way to spend a Saturday afternoon.

This was not a piece of trivia. It was the truth. Plus, it was eight days before Christmas.

Safta ran her fingers over the directory, looking at the list of clothing stores. "Is this it?" she asked. "A J.C. Penney and a suit shop? And a Gap? A gap is a hole. Who wants to buy clothes from a hole?"

"Chess King is a clothing store," I pointed out.

"It sounds like a game store."

I gave up. The mall was packed. Christmas carols blared from the speakers, making the air seem even stuffier.

I wished my mother had just ordered a suit from a catalog, or else taken me herself. But my grandmother said, "This time with David would be a gift." She made it hard to argue.

"I'm picking out his tie," my mother said.

"Can't you just buy something?" I asked my grandmother. "And I'll try it on at home?"

"No, no. We need a good fit. You don't want to look like Adam Goldberg, who didn't even tuck his shirt in, at his bar mitzvah. And the father? He looked like a schmuck and a half with ear flaps."

I didn't know what that even meant, but I knew I didn't want to look like one. I also didn't want to look like a guy who hung out at the mall with his grandmother. I had already seen some girls from my English class at the Hallmark store. Of course it was *some*, because it was a law that a girl couldn't be alone at the mall. She had to have at least one friend, preferably enough to make a pack.

I tried to walk far enough behind Safta so it didn't look like we were together, but that only made her turn around and tell me, loudly, to hurry up.

We tried J.C. Penney's first. "What kind of pants are these?" asked Safta, holding up a pair of gray pants and frowning. "Why are they so baggy? And who needs a zipper over the calf?"

"They're called parachute pants," I said. "They're really popular." I didn't want a pair of parachute pants—I was fine with jeans—but I felt obliged to defend them.

"Why are they called parachute pants? Because the only reason you'd wear them is if you were falling out of an airplane?" Safta flagged down a saleswoman. "Excuse me, where are your suits? You know, proper clothing for decent people?" A group of girls walking by giggled when she said that.

I looked away. And that's when I saw, at the far end of the store at the jewelry counter, Kelli Ann's best friend, Michelle.

My brain did the math: If Michelle was in J.C. Penney, and Michelle and Kelli Ann were best friends, then Kelli Ann was probably in J.C. Penney, too. And if Kelli Ann was in J.C. Penney and saw me with Safta, I was toast.

"Can we go?" I asked. Safta acted like she didn't even hear me. She dragged me to a back corner of the store, where the saleslady told her she could find suits for "little boys." I didn't mind going in that direction, because it was farther from the jewelry counter. But I didn't think a *little boy's* suit was what you should wear the day you are supposed to become a man. It turned out that the suits looked just like the suits my dad wore when he was forced to dress up, though.

Safta held up the largest one, in navy blue, against me.

"Could this one fit?" she asked. She made me turn around. I did, but I bent my knees, hoping that the clothing racks would provide some cover.

"Why are you squatting down? Stand up straight!" She was loud enough for the whole store to hear.

"Put on the jacket," commanded Safta. I tried to cram the suit jacket over my puffy winter coat.

"It'sfinecanwego?" I said.

Safta sighed. "David, stop this nonsense! Take off your winter coat and try it on properly."

I did what she told me, so that she would stop being so loud. The arms came down over my hands in a flappy way that made it look as though I didn't have any hands at all. Safta grabbed a jacket that was two sizes smaller.

"Turn around," she said. If I spun like that in PE, I would have gotten a better grade in our dance unit. "You know what? You really don't have much of a *tuchus*. It's flat, even for a boy your age. Maybe it's your Chinese genes."

If Kelli Ann only *heard* Safta, she would figure out it was me, because who else would talk about *tuchuses* and flat Chinese butts in the same sentence?

"Safta," I said, hoping to stop her before she could tell the whole store about the history of rear ends, and my rear end in particular. I tried to think of something that would make her stop. "Let's keep shopping. At other stores. I want to see all my choices and . . . I want to spend more time with you."

"More time with your little old safta?" She was practically purring. "This time is special for me, too. Oh, David, I wish I could have taken you to New York. Better selection, better prices . . ."

I poked my head up over the clothing racks and scanned the store. I didn't see Michelle at the jewelry counter anymore. Even better, there was a clear path from the boys department to the entrance to the mall.

"Okay, let's go." I felt as if I was in one of those war movies, where the hero is trying to get from one foxhole to another by speed and perfect timing. Safta just strolled behind me, oblivious to the danger around her.

The next shop was called Suitings. It only had men's clothes, which made me feel a lot safer about who I would run into there.

"Much better," she said. "And look at the selection!"

If by selection she meant varying shades of black, brown, gray, and blue, then yes, I guess she was right. But it all pretty much looked the same to me.

"So are we having a special occasion?" asked the salesman, whose nametag read JEAN-PAUL. I was betting he made up the "Jean" part so he'd sound French and expensive.

Safta smiled. "My grandson's bar mitzvah!"

"I see, I see." Jean-Paul took out a measuring tape and began holding it up to me. I felt like a piece of furniture.

"He's very small in the shoulders," said Jean-Paul. "That will limit us somewhat."

"He's built like his sister," agreed Safta.

I actually thought my shoulders were getting bigger from digging. Or maybe if I hadn't been digging, things would be worse.

"We can definitely rule out double-breasteds," said Jean-Paul. "Those are for men with more girth."

Safta nodded enthusiastically. "And have you noticed his *tuchus*? Like a pancake."

"We'll take good measurements," Jean-Paul assured her. "A good tailor is a miracle worker."

Based on their descriptions, I was starting to feel like the Hunchback of Eisenhower Junior High. Or a blue plate special. I couldn't wear dark colors, because that would make my small, girlish shoulders look even smaller. I should wear tan, they decided, with a narrow lapel.

"He needs all the help he can get," said Jean-Paul, apparently forgetting that I could hear him. "Here. Try this."

I put the jacket on, even though I was only wearing a T-shirt.

"You look like James Bond!" said Jean-Paul cheerfully. Because James Bond shopped with his grandmother at Suitings.

I stared at the mirror. Maybe I was stupid, for thinking that Kelli Ann could ever like me, homunculus that I was. Maybe she was only being nice to me out of pity.

I was broken out of my thoughts when I felt something *down there.* Jean-Paul was measuring me for the pants.

Was there no end to this?

"We have to be careful that the pants do not have too much fabric in that region," said Jean-Paul, snapping up his measuring tape.

"David?"

In the three-way mirror, there were three Kelli Anns, plus three Michelles, and nine other friends. Or was that three?

I briefly wondered if I could get away with pretending

that I was just someone who looked exactly like me, but wasn't. Safta nudged me. "David, honey, those girls are talking to you."

"Oh. Hi." Did Safta really have to call me *honey* in front of everyone? "What are you doing here?"

"I'm looking for a tie for my dad. For Christmas." She pointed at me, in my narrow-shouldered, pancake-butt glory. "What are you doing?"

Dying. I am dying.

"I'm setting a goot," I said, with as much dignity as I could muster.

"We're trying to find David a suit for his bar mitzvah," announced Safta. "Are you girls from David's school?"

"Totally," said Michelle. She said *totally* a lot.

I closed my eyes. *Dear Russians, if by chance you are presently planning to drop the bomb, please aim for Suitings at the Oak Faire Mall.*

"He is getting an *Arnauld Portier*," said Jean-Paul, putting some extra French flair on the name. "It's very nice."

That got the girls' attention. They nodded approvingly. And then Kelli Ann said something miraculous.

"You're having a bar mitzvah. That's like a party, right?" She smiled. "Fun." If you put all her words together, she almost said, *Your bar mitzvah sounds like fun!*

"Yes. It will be. Fun, I mean."

"C'mon, guys," whined one of her friends. "I don't want to shop for a tie. Let's go to Spencer's."

"Yeah, okay," agreed Kelli Ann. "Maybe I can get him a joke tie." They moved out of the store like a herd of deer. Kelli Ann wiggled her fingers at me.

I didn't exhale until they were all out of sight.

"*Jolie fille*, my friend," said Jean-Paul in an accent I'm pretty sure he made up, too. He clapped me on the shoulder. "You are a lucky guy."

I wouldn't exactly call myself *lucky* to have a group of girls catch me at Suitings. But then again, hearing Kelli Ann say that a bar mitzvah sounded like fun? That did seem sort of lucky.

"Are these girls on your invitation list?" asked Safta.

"Almost," I told her.

19

I spent the rest of Saturday hoping that Safta wouldn't say anything to my family. *I met some of David's little friends at the mall today!* Fortunately, she became obsessed with finding shoes for me, and by the time we got home, she was too tired to blab to anyone.

"I can't believe you guys went to the mall without me," complained Lauren. She had been at a basketball game when we left and was mad that Safta had taken me to the mall instead of cheering her on.

"That's all I needed," I said. "Another person watching Jean-Paul tell me I don't have a butt."

Lauren took a sofa pillow and threw it at me. "It's just all about what you want right now, isn't it? You and your butt?"

"Trust me, this is *not* what I wanted." I threw the pillow back at her. "What, you wanted more buttons?" Her button today was a picture of a red circle, with the words PRESS

HERE. Sometimes a button was just a button. Sometimes it meant the end of the world.

"No! Sheesh, those buttons."

"At least you're known for something," I said.

"You're known! The King of Trivia. Everyone thinks you're smart."

This was news to me. "They do?"

Lauren let out a long snort. "You beat the eighth graders. Even my English teacher knew." She picked at a piece of fuzz on the sofa. "You're known for something you can *do*."

"So are you."

Lauren looked at me, sadder than I think she meant to. "Wearing buttons isn't doing anything."

After all that, it was a relief to work on the hole on Sunday, even though the air was colder and the dirt was hard to pierce with our shovels. I started off in my coat, but in a few minutes I was sweating and I took it off. We had started a tunnel off the main hole, sort of like the way an elbow pipe looks in plumbing. Digging a tunnel was even harder than digging a regular hole, because first you had to scoop out the dirt sideways from the tunnel, and then you had to lift it up and out of the hole.

"What did you get for Hanukkah?" Scott asked as we were digging and hauling.

"Stuff," I said.

"What stuff?" he said.

"I got a couple of Atari games," I said.

"Which ones?"

I wanted to say, *ones that will never be as cool as the ones you're probably getting for Christmas*, but instead, I said, "E.T. and Dig Dug." Dig Dug seemed appropriate, because of all of the digging Scott and I were doing. So far, we hadn't encountered any monsters in our tunnel, though.

"Dig Dug's okay, I guess," Scott said. "E.T.'s not supposed to be any good."

"It isn't." My mom loved *E.T.*, and I thought the movie was okay. But the game was terrible. I was already tempted to throw it in the trash.

I tried to think of a way to bring up talking to girls.

I gave myself a C-plus for my conversation with Kelli Ann at the mall because, while I'd been able to convey a coherent thought, I lost points for sentence mangling. Scott didn't have this problem. When he talked to girls, he didn't mangle anything. He was in *control.*

"My sister got *Thriller*." You couldn't be an eleven-year-old in America and not expect to get *Thriller* this year, whatever holiday you were celebrating. Michael Jackson was for all people.

Scott grunted. Since only one of us could fit in the main hole, one person had to do most of the work, digging out the tunnel. The person at the top of the hole, which is where I was, had a lot less to do.

I tried again. "I'm just glad I didn't have to buy her a real present, 'cause girls are kind of hard to buy for, you know?" I'd gotten her a button, which I felt bad about in light of our earlier conversation.

This time Scott answered. "Naw. You just buy 'em some perfume and junk."

"What junk?"

"I don't know," Scott said. "Lip gloss or a unicorn or something."

"A *unicorn*?"

"Not a real unicorn," he said, like he couldn't believe what an idiot I was. "A stuffed one. Or ceramic."

What I really wanted to ask was *how do you talk to girls without sounding like you've lost your mind?* "Some girls don't seem like the unicorn type," I said. "Like, um, Kelli Ann Majors." I tried to say her name like I picked it out at random.

Scott grinned at me. "You like her, huh?"

"I didn't say that. I just said that she didn't seem like the unicorn type of girl."

"Yeah, sure."

I figured Scott could see right through me, so I decided to forge ahead. "So, when you see a girl, how do you approach her?" I liked the word *approach*. It reminded me of landing an airplane, which was way less scary than talking to a girl.

"You just say hi and their name. Like, Hi, Amanda."

"Then what?"

"They say hi back. It works every time. Well, almost every time."

"Um, okay." It seemed too easy.

"You want some real advice?" Scott said. "Stay away from girls. Be a lone wolf. Relationships make you weak." He handed me a bucket, dense with dirt. "Speaking of weak, did you get Hector? *My daddy's gonna let us watch an R-rated movie.*"

"He was just trying to be nice," I said.

"We're almost *thirteen*," said Scott. "We should be sneaking into R movies, not depending on someone's dad to rent one. Hector's a weak link. He'd never make it out here."

I didn't think Hector would be a weak link. But the thing was, we *were* on Scott's family's property. Maybe I was a weak link, too. I used to think of mushrooms only as a possible pizza topping, but now I pictured a huge, rolling mushroom cloud and winced.

I gave up on the girl conversation and changed it to school. There were girls at school. Maybe it would come up more naturally that way. "Did you start on your science project yet?" I asked him.

"No. But I'm thinking about doing something on survival."

"Oh, yeah, me too," I said. "How did you do on Hudson's test?" Mr. Hudson had given us a test on the Great Depression.

I could tell Scott was shrugging, even though he was shoveling at the same time.

"Do you know what you're going to do your paper on?"

More shrugging. "What about you?"

"Diplomacy?" Our assignment, which Mr. Hudson had told us about at the beginning of the term, was about the Cold War. Basically, he wanted us to solve it, like we were the UN. Points would be given for creativity and plausibility.

"We could blow them up," Scott said. "That would end it."

But that's what we didn't want to happen—"mutually assured destruction" and all that. Plus, I almost knew a Russian now, with Alexi, so joking about it didn't feel right. "I don't think Mr. Hudson would call that 'creative,'" I said.

"But it's plausible. And effective." Scott climbed out of the hole, and I jumped in.

I emptied a shovelful of dirt into a bucket. A millipede scurried out, and I could tell I'd damaged a few of its legs. That didn't seem to slow him down. He was red and prehistoric-looking. I watched him for a minute as he climbed down the bucket and back up the mud wall. I wondered if he would survive a nuclear war, like the cockroaches in *The Day After*. If he did, I wondered if they'd be friends.

"You know what's wrong with nuclear weapons?" I asked. I'd been thinking about this. "There are no heroes. It's not like in the previous wars where you threw yourself on a grenade or you took a hill even when the odds were against you. This time, it's just pressing a button and then seeing who's left."

Scott let out a strange laugh. "Yeah, well, once you're bent on destroying the other side, what do you expect?"

I went back to digging. Scott and I were preparing for the end of the world, but the difference was Scott didn't seem to care or even want to try to stop it.

If Hector were here, he'd probably mention that his favorite hero was Robin Hood. Or he'd name his favorite heroic moments in old war movies. Or maybe he wouldn't. But he definitely would not act like the end of the world was a sure thing.

"I have a Russian twin," I said. "Maybe I can write about that."

"You have a what?" Scott said.

"A Russian twin. It's not a real twin. Just somebody I got paired up with for my bar mitzvah. My grandmother got me into it. I don't even know him, but I'm writing to him. Maybe he can give me some information."

"You're communicating with Russians?"

"He hasn't written back," I said. "So it doesn't count as communicating. And it's not like that. He's one of the good guys."

"*We're* the good guys," Scott said.

"So is Alexi," I insisted. The shovel hit a rock and made a harsh, metallic sound. "He's being repressed by the Soviets. Because he's Jewish."

"He's probably just saying that to get your sympathy," said Scott. "I'll bet he's a spy."

Here's the weird thing: I didn't know Alexi from the

not-so-proverbial hole in the ground, but I felt as though I needed to protect him.

"It's all been checked out," I told Scott. "Alexi's the real deal." I used the shovel to try to feel for the edges of the rock, but it must have been a big one because everywhere I tapped was just more rock. "There's a rock in the way," I told Scott.

"So dig it out."

"No, it's big. Really big. I think digging it out could destabilize the tunnel."

"Look, we can't stop every time we run into something. We gotta commit. Dig it out." Scott was acting like the rock was my fault.

At one point in *The Great Escape*, part of the tunnel falls down on one of the diggers, showering him with dirt. Not super bad, but enough that he had to be helped out, and I wondered if moving the rock might do the same thing. If I told that to Scott, he would think I was a worrywart. "I'll get started," I said. "But this is definitely a two-man job, okay?"

Scott gave me a weird look. "Two people can't even fit in the tunnel."

I thought of a different reason to have two people. "I think we'll need two people to get the rock out of the hole."

"Yeah, sure," said Scott. Then he started doing a weird dance around the hole. "*Da*, comrade. We vill remove all rocks from ze motherland!" He saluted. "Is that how your Commie pen pal talks?"

"I told you, he hasn't written back yet," I said. "It probably takes a long time to get letters past the censors and all that."

"He's probably a spy, trying to infiltrate young American minds," said Scott. "Aw, blow 'em all back to the Stone Age. Who has time to sort them all out?"

Anger rushed over me. Here I was, trying to be reasonable and he couldn't even take two seconds to admit that maybe I was right. And making fun of Alexi wasn't okay, either. I wanted to say *dig your own dumb tunnel*. But I needed it to be my tunnel, too. And maybe a tunnel for Hector or my family or Kelli Ann. "I gotta go," I said, before I could say anything else.

I walked halfway back to my house before I remembered I'd left my jacket near the hole. I didn't want to go back for it, though. I went straight to my room and pulled out a piece of paper. My fingers were stiff from the cold, so my handwriting was pretty lousy.

Dear Alexi,

I haven't heard from you yet. I guess you're busy, being repressed and all.

When we read about the Soviet Union at school, we usually learn that Moscow is the capital and that you just got a new leader, Andropov (I think I spelled that right).

They show us pictures of St. Basil's Cathedral with the onion tops. They don't tell us much about what kids do in Russia, but you probably have normal stuff, like school and friends.

One of my best friends is Scott. He is normally pretty cool.

I stopped and I wondered if I should tell Alexi that Scott and I had a fight about him. Or a non-fight. Alexi would probably think Scott was a jerk if he found out that Scott wanted to blow him up. So I decided to say something more general. Now I was covering for Scott. I wrote:

Sometimes he has some pretty strange ideas.

I reread my letter. Mr. Haggerty, my English teacher, was always telling us to do that. I decided that I needed to end on a more positive note.

Tonight is the third night of Hanukkah, which means that it's socks and underwear night, at least in our house.

I thought about writing about the two video games, but decided against it. Maybe getting socks and underwear for Hanukkah would be a big deal in Russia. Maybe they didn't get to celebrate at all.

My social studies teacher, Mr. Hudson, wants us to write a paper about how to solve the Cold War—that's what we call the thing that's going on between the US and the Soviet Union—in our country. Is that what you call it, too? Do you have any ideas?

Maybe I should have asked if he had any ideas about how to talk to girls, too. But somehow, asking about how to solve the Cold War seemed easier.

Socks and underwear night turned out to be pretty fun, aside from the socks and underwear. I finally figured out how to spin the dreidel on its stem instead of the normal way. When I was little and my Grandpa Joe was still alive, he'd do it. But I could never do it myself. The trick was to spin the dreidel and kind of snap your fingers at the same time, and to face your hand up instead of down.

"Look, Safta." I flicked the dreidel so that it spun on its stem.

Safta watched it spin until it fell over. It landed on *shin*, which is the worst letter you can get. But that wasn't the point and my grandmother knew it.

"Your grandpa would be proud," she said. I could tell she missed him. Safta was different when Grandpa Joe was alive. She'd still try to get her way, but Grandpa Joe could always get her not to take things so seriously.

Wai Po joined us for the present opening. She gave Lauren and me dress socks and spun the dreidel. Then she told us about the *da touluo,* a top-spinning competition in China.

"Tops *come* from China," she said. "China invented them."

I lifted up my dreidel and studied it closely. It said *Made in Taiwan,* but Wai Po would say that didn't matter—it was still Chinese.

I peeked over at Safta to see if she would say something back, but she just smiled and said, "Isn't that nice?"

Why couldn't it always be like this? I'll never understand why people get along sometimes, and fight other times. I wish I did. I bet I could solve a lot of problems that way. Maybe even big problems, like the Cold War.

At the beginning of the week, posters appeared all

over the hall. *Science Fair! Monday!* A lot of the posters had little beakers drawn around the edges, and a volcano in the middle, because whoever made the posters knew that 50 percent of the kids would make vinegar-baking soda volcanoes.

Our school always has the science fair on a Monday night, so you have a weekend to get your project together. The fair was optional when you were in sixth grade, but required when you were in seventh. Mrs. Osterberg made a big point of saying that if our experiment didn't work, it was fine, as long we documented the reasons why.

"That's science," she continued. "What was it Edison said? *'I have not failed; I've just found 10,000 ways that won't work.'*"

She looked at us and added, "Indeed." Then she scrawled the quote on the board, only no one could read it. In my experience, English teachers have good handwriting; science teachers don't. Anyway, it didn't matter what she wrote up there because nobody listened to that bit of advice for the science fair. We believed in another saying: *If your science experiment fails, it's time to go find a new science experiment.*

I wrote up a bunch of ideas, all of which had to do with what would help us survive longer in the event of a nuclear attack. My best idea was: *find out whether tuna fish or Spam gives you more energy over the long term.* We couldn't stock fresh food in the shelter; it had to be stuff in cans, and based on how much we'd dug out so far, it couldn't take up a lot of room. We had to choose wisely. I didn't have time for the "long-term" part of my experiment, but I figured a few days would be enough for Mrs. O.

The only problem was I needed test subjects.

"Come on," I said to Scott that afternoon. I decided to help him dig, even though I was still ticked off at him. The opening to the tunnel was getting bigger, but we still couldn't get the rock out.

"You're dreaming," he said. He seemed mad at me, too, but the only thing he said was: "Spam is repulsive."

"That might be all we have to eat if there's a bomb," I said. "This is for science." And then, as if it wasn't obvious, "*And* our survival."

Half of Scott disappeared into the tunnel. Then some dirt flew out, followed by Scott (crawling, not flying). He lifted out a mound of dirt that was mingled with a layer of red Virginia clay. He had a spray of dirt in his hair. "There's no way I'm eating Spam," he said. "But I might eat the tuna."

That was as good as a *yes*, but I still needed a subject to try the Spam (consumed by more people in Hawaii than in any other state). For about two seconds, I thought about asking Kelli Ann just so we'd have something to talk about. But Spam didn't seem like the sort of thing I wanted her to associate with me. That left Hector. I felt guilty about asking him to eat Spam when we weren't even going to allow him into our bomb shelter, but weirdly, Hector sounded thrilled.

"No problem. But only for three days, right?"

"Just three. You'll be doing great things for science."

"Yeah. Me and Albert Einstein," he said. "Remind me again. What's your scientific purpose?" The scientific purpose was the question we wanted to explore in the project.

I hesitated. If I told Hector exactly the reason why, it might lead to a discussion about the bomb shelter, which he didn't even know existed. And then I would have to explain why he wasn't out there digging with us. "I want to study the effects of a limited diet," I said, which was technically true. Then, to make it sound more scientific, "The physical and psychological effects of a limited diet."

But in my brain, I thought about the physical and psychological effects of lying to my best friend. Stomach weirdness? Check. Also, my skin felt colder. Sure, Hector could be immature and embarrassing sometimes, but I'd nearly forgotten that he was usually up for anything, like eating only Spam for three days. And that he didn't make a big deal out of it, either. Even though I was guessing that tuna gave you more energy than Spam, I hoped that with the experiment, Hector would show Scott that he wasn't soft, and that he deserved a spot in the shelter.

DWIGHT D. EISENHOWER SCIENCE FAIR WORKSHEET

Fill in each section with complete sentences. Think about the scientific process as we discussed it in class, and apply it to your project.

TITLE OF PROJECT: *The Physical and Psychological Effects of a Limited Diet on Adolescents*

SCIENTIFIC QUESTION: *What works better as a limited diet: canned tuna fish or canned ham (Spam)?*

INTRODUCTION (Please explain why you chose this experiment, if you were assisted by anyone, and any preliminary research you conducted): *After watching* The Day After, *in which many people are forced to seek shelter without access to their regular resources, I wanted to know which of two food sources would best sustain humans. I was assisted by Scott Dursky (Subject A) and Hector Clelland (Subject B). My research* consisted of going to the store and figuring out what kind of protein food had a long shelf life and could last in post-nuclear conditions. I also needed to find a food that fit within my budget. According to the manufacturers, tuna and Spam (unopened) have a shelf life of up to five years.

HYPOTHESIS (This is your guess of what you think will happen during the experiment, and why): I think the subject who consumes tuna will do better because it is less gross than Spam, thus that subject will eat more of it.

MATERIALS: Spam (canned ham), tuna, weights, track, stopwatch, and math worksheets from Mrs. Fink's fourth-period class

PROCEDURE: (Write the steps to your experiment so that another person could conduct your experiment independently, by following your instructions.)

1. Have the subjects lift weights, run a mile, and complete math worksheets. Record the data.

2. Give Subject A three cans of tuna. Give Subject B three cans of Spam. This is all they get to eat for the next three days, plus water. When Subject B complains that he didn't know that tuna was an

option, explain that you need something for comparison.

3. After one day of the canned food—only diet, have the subjects lift weights, run a mile, and complete math worksheets again. Record the data. Try not to worry that Subject B looks like he's going to pass out during the mile run. Don't listen to Subject A when he says that Subject B is a "weak link." Also write down subjective data, i.e., how the subjects say they feel.

4. On day two, repeat step 3. During lunch, hide the nice roast beef sandwich that your mom made for you and eat it later.

5. On day three, repeat step 3. When you are done recording all the data, tell the subjects that they are free to resume a normal diet.

RESULTS: Use a table or graph to best display your data and results.

Moods of Subjects

	Subject A	Subject B
Before	Fine	Fine
Day 1	Bored	Not so great
Day 2	Okay	Better than yesterday — things are weirdly clear
Day 3	Bored	A little tired — Looking forward to food

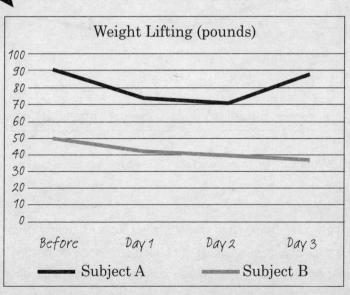

Weight Lifting (pounds)

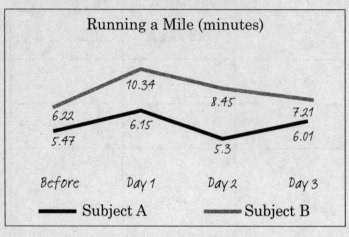

Running a Mile (minutes)

- 6.22
- 10.34
- 8.45
- 7.21
- 5.47
- 6.15
- 5.3
- 6.01

Before | Day 1 | Day 2 | Day 3

— Subject A   ▬ Subject B

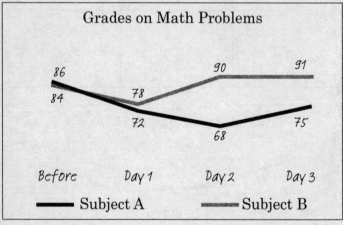

Grades on Math Problems

- 86
- 84
- 78
- 72
- 90
- 91
- 68
- 75

Before | Day 1 | Day 2 | Day 3

— Subject A   ▬ Subject B

DISCUSSION: What do your results show? If your data is inconclusive, explain why.

You would think that, overall, tuna worked better than Spam. Subject A actually performed better on weightlifting on Day 3, while Subject B lifted fewer and fewer weights every day. Also, Subject A did not lose much time on the mile run, while Subject B had a lot of variation, but remember, Subject A has the school record for the mile run. Subject B did do better on the math problems than Subject A, but Subject A did not seem to be trying very hard.

However, there is one big problem with all of this. It turns out that Subject A was eating other food the whole time.*

CONCLUSION:

Subject A is a jerk.

*Foods Eaten By Subject A in Addition to Tuna Fish: Hamburger, mac and cheese, cereal (times three), milk (times three), ham sandwich, peanut butter sandwich, potato chips, pretzels, Little Debbie Snack Cake, chocolate chip cookies, Rice Krispy Treats, rice, beans, peanut butter toast, egg, Hostess Cupcakes.

I rewrote the conclusion before I turned in my paper.
Even though it was true, I didn't think that's what Mrs.
Osterberg was looking for.

Here's what happened: I'd just finished recording all the
data and told Scott and Hector that they could have regular
dinners; I was done.

Hector's face lit up. "Really? 'Cause my mom is making
empanadas. I've been dreaming about food every night."

That made me feel worse. Even though he hadn't complained so much, Hector had been really, really hungry the
whole time.

"You should probably eat a double portion," I said as
Hector turned toward his house. Scott and I lived in the
other direction.

Out of the corner of my eye, I could see Scott roll his
eyes. Then his expression changed to a smile, and I saw that
Kelli Ann and her friends were just ahead of us.

I decided to try Scott's advice. "Hi, Kelli Ann!"

She turned around. "Hi," she said. They slowed down so we could catch up.

"See?" Scott said. "It works."

Kelli Ann was holding a foil-lined shoe box. "You want a Rice Krispy treat? It's Michelle's birthday."

We reached in the box, but then Kelli Ann slapped away Scott's hand, sort of playfully. "Not you, you pig!" she said. "You've already had two! Anyway, there will be more snacks when you come to my house tonight."

Scott turned about nine shades of purple.

I looked from Kelli Ann to Scott, and then back again. Two thoughts crowded into my brain. Scott cheated on my experiment. Scott was going to Kelli Ann's house.

Scott smiled as if nothing was wrong. I wondered if there was a way to strangle him without Kelli Ann noticing.

"Thanks for the Rice Krispy treat," I said to Kelli Ann. At least I managed to talk normally.

I thought back to my conversation with Scott, the one where I'd left Hector behind so I could ask about girls.

Be a lone wolf, he said. *Relationships make you weak.*

That wasn't advice. It was Scott strategically arranging to have Kelli Ann all for himself.

I turned for home. Scott said something else to Kelli Ann. "Wait up," he called to me. I pretended not to hear him and walked faster.

"Dude, just do another experiment," he said after he caught up.

"No," I said. "I did this one." I was acting like I was mad at Scott for messing up my experiment, and I was. But Scott messing around with Kelli Ann bothered me more.

"You know what's the worst thing?" I added, though really, it wasn't the worst thing, not even close. "You cheated today and did worse on the test. My hypothesis was that tuna would give you more energy. But now it looks like the Rice Krispy treats sucked it away."

"You really need a bigger sample size if you want to be scientific," Scott said. "You know that, right?"

Shut up about the sample size! I thought. I tried to figure out how to salvage the experiment. "Okay, you ate today. I can still use the results from the first two days."

"Here's the thing," Scott said. He didn't finish his sentence, letting me fill in the blanks.

"You ate something else?"

Scott didn't look at me. He just started mumbling some names of food. *Cereal, ham sandwich, potato chips, Little Debbie Snack Cake . . .*

It turned out Scott didn't even skip breakfast the very first morning. And when I thought he was eating tuna for lunch he'd already eaten a ham sandwich. Scott, who had said Hector would be a weak link to our survival, didn't do the experiment *at all*.

"Did you even stick to the diet for five minutes?" I asked him.

"I got hungry," Scott said.

"If you couldn't hack it, you shouldn't have said you'd do it."

"It's a junior high school science experiment, okay? You aren't going to revolutionize our knowledge of nutrition. The government probably has whole departments dedicated to that kind of research."

"That's not the point. This was *my* research. I was trying to do something to help us survive in the shelter," I said. *Unlike your experiment,* I thought, but didn't say. Instead of doing something on survival, Scott ended up doing the vinegar-and-baking soda volcano like everybody else.

If I said the things I really wanted to, Scott and I were through, that much I knew. I would be giving up my survival space. I tried counting to ten. In health, that's what they taught us to do when we felt mad. I counted by twos.

"*You* didn't try to eat tuna for three days," said Scott, who apparently still thought the experiment was the only issue. "You don't know what it's like."

"You know what?" I said. "You don't, either."

I thought that if I didn't say anything, I would stop

feeling mad at Scott, and then I wouldn't *have* to say anything. There were a couple of times I saw him in the hall where I pretended not to see him. Sort of like I used to with Kelli Ann, except I really did want to talk to Kelli Ann, and did *not* want to talk to Scott. At all. Especially after I got my grade on my science project. Mrs. Osterberg gave me a C-minus.

"A nice thought but not enough of a sample for a true scientific comparison," she wrote. "Good graphs and useful question, but if you had a bigger sample size you would have been able to draw some sort of conclusion when Subject A deviated. You should have tried this experiment across genders, as well."

When Subject A deviated. She meant when Scott cheated. And I guess I *should* have asked Kelli Ann—that would have solved the gender question. Not that it would have helped me in the way I wanted it to, since Kelli Ann and Scott were a *thing*.

I still sat next to him in English, but I didn't do any more than the bare minimum. Say hello. Pass the quiz on *A Separate Peace*.

Mr. Haggerty was wearing a super-bad tie, green with cartoon children on it. (The average silk necktie requires about one hundred and twenty silkworm cocoons. But Mr. Haggerty's ties were mostly cotton.) Scott passed me a note. *Nice tie. Nice* was underlined three times. I nodded and slid the note back to him. I had never been so intent on doing well on one of Mr. Haggerty's quizzes.

The note slid back. *Want to come over today?*

Can't.

As in, *I can't because I have my lesson with Rabbi Doug.* I didn't write *won't*, as in *won't because you're a jerk*, but I was thinking that, too.

Scott gave me a funny look, one eyebrow lifted and one corner of his mouth curled slightly. I pretended not to see, or understand.

During my bar mitzvah practice, I tried to look as though nothing was bothering me. I didn't do such a good job because Rabbi Doug figured me out in about five minutes.

"Is something bothering you, David?"

I fiddled with my *chumash*, which is basically a

bound-up, printed version of the Torah. It's easier to read because it's a book, not a scroll. Plus, there are vowels.

"No," I said. I didn't think I was supposed to lie to a rabbi, though, so I added, "Not exactly."

"Ah." Rabbi Doug stood up and straightened a picture on the wall. "Well, the thing is, your chanting is not going so well today. I was thinking that if you were distracted that might explain it. Otherwise, I might need to talk to your parents about increasing your practice time." He didn't look at me when he said this. He was staring very intently at his picture of a tree—the tree of life, maybe.

Rabbi Doug was saying, *Tell me what's wrong, kid, or get more homework.*

"There's this friend," I began.

"Mmm-hmm."

"Did you see *The Day After*?"

"I did," he said. So I told him the rest.

For someone who spends most of his time talking *to* people, Rabbi Doug was surprisingly good at listening. He didn't interrupt. He made little listening noises. Sometimes he agreed with me, like when I told him about Scott messing up my science experiment. (He made a face about the Spam part, and I don't think it was just because Spam wasn't kosher.)

"He didn't keep his word," said Rabbi Doug.

"Exactly! What if we hadn't run into Kelli Ann? I

wouldn't have known anything. My results would have been totally fake."

"You're angry."

"He *lied* to me. He messed up my science experiment. I'm supposed to wait out a nuclear war with this guy?"

"What about Hector?"

"No, I was talking about Scott." I guess all these names were kind of confusing for Rabbi Doug. "Scott's the one who lied to me."

"I know." Rabbi Doug spun around in his chair and leaned back. "But who lied to Hector?"

My face turned hot. I hadn't told Rabbi Doug specifically about leaving Hector out, but I guess he figured it out. "I just left out some details." As the words came out, though, I could hear how thin they were. "A lot of details," I added.

"When you *leave out the details*, as you say, do you respect yourself?" asked Rabbi Doug.

I thought about all the times I'd told Hector I was doing something else, and how I didn't tell him everything about my science experiment, even though he was basically willing to starve for three days. For me.

I shook my head. "I was thinking about surviving," I said.

"Think about this, David," said Rabbi Doug. "What if you really did have to start over in the world? How would you want to start?"

He started saying something about dishonesty and deception and how both were crimes under Jewish law, but I was already ahead of him. I knew.

"That's enough for today," Rabbi Doug said, looking at his watch. "Maybe it will give you some inspiration for your bar mitzvah speech. And for Hector."

As soon as I got home, I called Hector. I started out by apologizing for the botched science experiment.

"That's okay, I guess," he said. "Though you could have eaten the Spam yourself. Then I could have eaten the tuna and you would have gotten accurate results."

"I couldn't eat the Spam. It was my experiment; I was the scientist."

"So?" said Hector. "Jonas Salk gave himself and his whole family the polio shot as an experiment."

"True," I said.

"I can't believe I ate Spam for you for three days for nothing." He didn't sound mad at me—just mad that his sacrifice didn't contribute to any lasting results.

But I hadn't gotten to the leaving-you-out-of-the-survival-plan part of my apology yet. And that's when I realized that Scott had been wrong about something else. Sure, the strong (and the cockroaches) would probably be the most likely to survive a nuclear attack. But if I was going to be stuck starting over again in a messed-up world, I would want to start over with someone who was more than just strong. I would want to start over with a guy who was willing to eat Spam for me for three days when he didn't even have to. I would want to start over with a real friend.

Not Scott. I was never sure why Seal and my grandmother had never made up after all those years. But suddenly, not speaking to someone ever again didn't seem so crazy; it seemed like a good idea.

"Come over after dinner tonight," I told Hector. "I've got something to show you."

Dinner took forever. My parents were arguing, again, about my bar mitzvah.

"She doesn't think I can do it," my mother told my father. "She doesn't trust me because I'm Chinese. She keeps second-guessing me."

I wanted to tell her that Safta second-guessed everybody, even the rabbi. But I kept my mouth shut.

"We are really short on time," my father said. "Let her keep helping. It would be—"

"A gift," my mother said. "I know."

Wai Po sat at the table, smiling a little. Then she frowned. "I think Bao Bao is looking a little heavy," she said.

Now that she mentioned it, he did seem to be getting bigger. I wondered if that meant his poop was getting bigger, too. She smiled at him. "*Xiao pangzi.*"

"What does that mean?" I asked.

"Little fatso." I'd never heard the word *fatso* said so

lovingly. I wondered if she had a similarly flattering nickname for me that I didn't know about.

The phone rang. Mom picked it up. I hoped it was Hector.

"David," she said, putting her hand over the receiver. "Have you seen Scott? Did he say what he was doing after school today?"

I kept chewing my dinner and shook my head. Maybe he was hanging out with Kelli Ann, but I wasn't going to say *that*.

"I'm sorry, Marie. David hasn't seen him. We'll let you know if he shows up here." Mom set the phone back in the cradle. "Marie said Scott never showed up for dinner."

"He's fine," I said. "He's pretty good at looking out for himself."

When Hector came over, Mom said we could go out for forty-five minutes.

"Forty-five minutes? Why not an hour?" I asked.

"It's a school night, and it'll be pitch-black in forty-five minutes," Mom said, as if the fifteen minutes really mattered. "Maybe you can check some of the places Scott usually goes. His mother sounded really worried."

I grabbed my jacket and a flashlight.

"What's up with Scott?" Hector asked as soon as we got out of the house.

"Who knows?" I said.

"Where are we going?" Hector asked.

"Just trust me." We hurried down the road. The sun was mostly down, and though it was easy to see Hector and cars and trees and stuff, it was hard to make out the colors of anything. Dusk was one of those words like cricket knees. When you said it over and over, it didn't sound like anything.

"But Scott's missing?" Hector said.

"He probably went to Kelli Ann's." I could say it to Hector, though it still hurt.

"Are they together?" He sounded surprised. "*Together* together?"

I shrugged and kept walking. A plan started to form in my mind. Hector and I would dig our own survival hole and leave out Scott. Our hole would be better because neither of us were jerks. And we could include anyone we wanted.

"Where are we?" Hector asked as we reached Scott's property and started up the driveway.

"So, remember that movie *The Day After*?"

"I wish I could forget it." Hector kicked the gravel. "Uh, do you know who lives here?"

"Sort of." It occurred to me that if I was mad at Scott, I probably shouldn't be trespassing on his family's property. But then again, Scott didn't play by the rules; maybe I shouldn't worry about them, either.

"So Scott and I had this idea about what to do, you know, if an actual bomb goes off. And, well . . ." At this point, my intention was to say something like *ta-da!* and show Hector the shelter. But when I flicked my flashlight toward the hole, like a spotlight, all the words flew out of my head.

Next to the hole leading down to the tunnel was a large, dirt-covered rock. And next to the rock, spread out like a puddle on the dark earth, was Scott's Members Only jacket.

"Scott!"

I was speaking to him again. I yelled his name but I didn't hear an answer.

"Come on," I told Hector. I ran toward the hole. In the dusk, it was hard to see the exact contour of the ground, but something was wrong.

"Scott, come on, your mom's looking for you!" I shouted.

"Where is he?" Hector asked. Then he spotted the hole.

We slowed down as we approached the edge. Usually, it was like looking into a manhole, with our tunnel extending out like a sewer pipe. I shined my flashlight down there, and caught, in the beam, Scott Dursky. All we could see was his head, turned to the side, and one arm stretching out. The rest of him was covered in dirt.

"Scott?"

The hand moved. I think. "Dave?" Usually he called me

David. It was as if he didn't have the strength to get out the second syllable.

"Hector's here, too," I said. "Come on. Get out of there." I tried to use the same tone of voice that Scott sometimes used with us. Tough with an edge of I-don't-care.

"Can't."

"Just crawl out," Hector said.

Scott pushed against the ground awkwardly with his free hand. Nothing happened. I heard another sound, like breathing, only not.

"Stop fooling around." I looked at Hector. "He's just messing around."

But then another sound came, a real one, the kind that let me know he wasn't fooling.

Scott Dursky was crying. Or at least, trying to cry between little gasps, like an untied balloon running out of air.

"Help me," he said.

I squatted so I could climb down, too, but Hector grabbed my arm. "Careful!" he warned. "The hole could go. It could all go." Even as his words hung in the air, a trickle of dirt fell like rain—or hail—and hit Scott's head.

I took another step back. "We've got to get some help." I looked at the house, but the windows were all dark. And then, even though I really *had* been sure I wasn't speaking to him anymore, I added, "Don't worry. You're going to be okay."

"No!" Scott turned his head slightly, trying to see me out

of the corner of his eye. "Don't leave." Then he added, "Please." It was not a Scott Dursky sort of word.

"Okay," I told him. "I'll stay here, and Hector will go for help."

Hector looked at me, wide-eyed. "I was following you. I'm not sure I can even find my way back." He whispered so Scott wouldn't hear him.

I talked louder. It's a trick I learned from Rabbi Doug: Your voice doesn't shake as much when it's loud. "Oops, reverse that. Hector will stay here, and I'll go get some help."

"NO!" Scott said. "If I'm going to die . . ."

"Nobody is dying, okay?" I swallowed hard and looked at the dirt we'd cleared out of the hole and piled into a mound a few feet away. I remembered how heavy each load was. If each bucket of dirt weighed eight to ten pounds, how much did the dirt weigh that was left? I was good at math, but I wasn't thinking clearly enough to do the calculations. I couldn't even think of how many loads were trapping Scott in the ground. "I won't be gone that long."

Scott curled his hand into a fist and thumped it into the ground. "Should have supported it," he said. "Happened fast." He choked back a sob.

Yes, we should have supported it. I knew it, too. I knew the cave-in was possible. Probable, even, according to *The Great Escape*. But I hadn't pushed harder. I hadn't said anything at all, after Scott said Virginia clay was safe. I hadn't said anything, even though I'd worried about the rock. I'd just dipped the shovel into the dirt and dug, because I didn't want Scott to think I was a wimp.

I zipped my jacket. "I'm going to make a run for it," I told Hector. "I'll stop at the first house with a light and call 911. Keep talking to him so he doesn't lose it."

"What are we going to talk about?" Hector asked. That stopped me. What would Scott and Hector talk about? The fact that Scott cheated on the science experiment? Or that Scott and I had been digging a shelter without Hector, leaving him to die if there was a nuclear disaster? That we were supposed to be a team?

I slipped my hand in my jacket pocket, and my fingers touched the edge of a stack of Trivial Pursuit cards. I'd started carrying them instead of my trivia book since they were even smaller. I pulled them out.

"Here," I said, slapping the pack into his hand. "Ask him these."

I started running, trying to avoid branches that kept slapping me in the face. I mentally mapped the street in my head. Where was the closest occupied house? At the corner of Armistead and Trotter? Or was that one still empty?

Once I hit the gravel driveway, the running got a bit easier. It took forever to reach the road. In the distance, I could see the headlights of a car.

I screamed as loud as I could and raised my hands. "Hey! Help! HELP!" It felt as though my words were disappearing into the air, but amazingly, the car turned and started up the driveway. The headlights temporarily blinded me.

Suddenly, I had this weird thought, that maybe this could be a psycho killer who prowled rural roads, searching for panicky-looking kids.

But a man I recognized as Scott's dad jumped out of the car. They had the same face, though Mr. Dursky was taller.

"David! What are you doing here?"

I wanted to ask him the same question, but then I remembered, they owned the house. "Scott's trapped in a hole in the back."

If Scott's dad was surprised by this, he didn't show it. "Take me to him."

"We can't get him out," I said. "Even with you. We need more help. We've got to get to a phone." The words couldn't come out fast enough. Somehow, I didn't mess any of them up.

Mr. Dursky reached into his car and pulled out a big rectangular object. "I'll call 911."

"We need a phone," I repeated wildly. Time seemed to be going in slow motion. I wanted Mr. Dursky to move faster, to run to the house, unlock the door, and make the call.

Mr. Dursky pulled a thin wire from the boxy-looking thing. An antenna. "David, this is a phone."

It took six firemen to get Scott out. They said that if

we had taken any longer to get help it could've been really bad.

Scott was already moaning a lot, so I didn't want to know how much worse "really bad" could be. I had my suspicions, though.

"What were you thinking?" Mr. Dursky kept asking. "What were you kids doing?"

I couldn't blame Mr. Dursky for thinking it was the three of us. I felt bad for Hector, who was getting blamed for this when he wasn't even a part of the digging. And for Scott, who might have been able to answer, but who didn't because of the moaning and because he was having trouble breathing. That left me to say that we were trying to save ourselves. But I didn't say it, because by trying to save ourselves, we had nearly killed Scott.

Scott was on the stretcher being loaded into the ambulance when his mom raced up in her car.

"Scott!" she cried, bending down to hug him, even though the paramedics said to watch out for his ribs. Mrs. Dursky had one of those huge perms, and it looked like a cloud of hair was attacking Scott.

After she had decided that Scott was not going to die, Mrs. Dursky turned on Mr. Dursky. "Is this what you've been letting him do all these weeks when you have visitation?"

Visitation?

"For Pete's sake, Marie, he's almost thirteen. I'm not going to watch him every minute." Mr. Dursky didn't look at her when he spoke.

"Well, that worked out really well, didn't it? Your only son nearly got himself killed." Mrs. Dursky's voice went up an octave, piercing the air. "He was supposed to be with me tonight."

Nearly killed, I kept saying in my head. Nearly. Now that didn't sound like a real word, either.

"Let's all calm down," said the paramedic. He had a reassuring voice, like my dad's.

"He's going to be okay," Mr. Dursky said. Then he added, "The cellular phone came in handy."

Scott's mom snorted. "You'd think that if you have money for a cellular telephone you could pay your child support."

Visitation. Child support. Those words meant divorce, which Scott had never managed to mention to me during all the hours we were digging.

I looked over at Scott in the back of the ambulance. He had one of those shiny emergency blankets wrapped around him, and it crinkled every time he moved. But there was no way he couldn't hear them. Everyone could.

Mrs. Dursky turned to me and Hector.

"I'm so glad you found him," she said. It was like we really had gone looking for him after she called our house. "You're real heroes. You saved him."

Except I didn't feel like a hero. It wasn't like the poison ivy. I'd almost killed him by being too chicken to argue with him about the rock. And we wouldn't have come out here at all if I hadn't wanted to come clean to Hector.

Mr. and Mrs. Dursky said they would follow the ambulance to the hospital. They took separate cars and left Hector and me standing alone in the empty driveway of what I now knew was not a rental property; it was where Mr. Dursky lived.

"Wow," said Hector.

"Yeah," I said. "Wow."

We started walking back to my house. Mr. Dursky had let me use his phone to call my parents, who said they would call Hector's parents. The connection was a little crackly, like when you talk into a walkie-talkie. Dad had offered to pick us up, but this was one of those times when walking seemed better. I wanted to talk to Hector.

"The hole," I said, not sure where to start. I never did get a chance to tell Hector what was going on with the hole.

"You guys have been digging for a while, I guess."

I didn't think I could feel worse about lying to Hector all of those weeks. I was wrong.

"Yeah."

Hector kicked a rock. It bounced under a streetlight and then into the darkness. "Clubhouse?" he asked.

"It was supposed to be a fallout shelter," I said. "But it fell in instead." Hector didn't laugh. I didn't blame him.

"A fallout shelter," he repeated.

"Just in case," I said.

"So you'd be safe." The way he said it, I knew he saw the whole picture, and not just part of it. He hadn't been invited to dig. He had definitely not been invited to live in the hole. It would have just been me, Scott Dursky, and the cockroaches.

"You know, I was never sure about Scott," Hector said. "I used to be sure about you, though. We were best friends." Hector has always said how he really felt about things.

Sometimes I liked that about him. But not always. Not now. He took a deep breath. "We've always done stuff together. Always. And now I don't even know you anymore."

I would have felt better if Hector had sounded angry. Instead, he just sounded sad.

It looked as though our friendship wasn't going to survive a nuclear war; it wasn't even going to survive the preparation for one.

When the Emergency Broadcast System told us this was

just a test, it was saying, *this didn't count*. And I guess you could argue that everything we were doing, digging the hole and trying out food, didn't matter unless the Russians actually attacked—until then, it was all practice. But it didn't feel that way. It was the other way around—the way we acted now mattered most.

We turned the corner to my street, and I could see the lights on in my house.

"I guess you knew about Scott's parents," he said.

"No," I said. "I had no idea." Maybe that's why Scott started to hang out with us; because we didn't know the difference, and he could pretend everything was normal. "You want to come in? My dad'll drive you home."

Hector shook his head. "No, thanks. I can make it on my own."

"You can have my flashlight," I told him.

"No, thanks," said Hector, a little too politely.

"No, really." I held it out to him. "You should take it. You can give it back later." I had this weird thought, which was that if Hector took the flashlight, it meant he wouldn't stay mad at me. He'd have to talk to me again.

Hector made a face and took the flashlight, and then I stood at the front door and watched Hector walk down the street as the light from the flashlight got smaller and smaller. I felt just like that flashlight.

When I got inside, Mom and Dad were waiting for me.

Mom hugged me first. "We were so worried!" she said. "Are you okay?"

"What's the word on Scott?" said Dad.

I shook my head. "I don't know." The image of Scott on the stretcher flashed in front of me.

"If he's at Commonwealth, I can find out," said Dad.

"So, Scott got trapped in a hole? I don't understand. Was this a hole from construction? A hole for . . . bears?" asked Mom. "What were you even doing out there?"

I didn't know how to begin to answer, so I didn't.

The next day at school, everyone was talking about

Scott and the fallout shelter. Heather Roberts came up to me in English and told me that she'd heard that we had a television in the shelter and that we'd wired our tunnel for electricity. It was the first time she'd ever spoken to me voluntarily.

"What are you guys going to do about the trivia contest?" she asked. "Can Scott even play, now that he's, you know?" She talked about him like he was dead instead of temporarily injured.

"His brain isn't hurt," I said. "Just ribs and stuff."

I wondered if people were talking to Hector about the shelter, except Hector didn't wait for me at the track in PE. We kept running on opposite sides of the oval, no matter how much I sped up or slowed down. He didn't show up at our regular lunch table, either. He must have gone to the library.

When I got home from school, Safta started bugging me—again—for my list of friends for the bar mitzvah. "Including those girls from the mall." She'd already mailed the invitations to out-of-town guests, the people who had to make plane reservations. She'd even mailed Seal an invitation.

I wanted to say *what's the point?* What was the point of even having a big bar mitzvah, if the only two friends I had weren't going to be there? But I didn't. I just told her that I'd get her a list.

I checked the mail. Alexi hadn't written back, so he didn't even feel like a real person. But he was the only friend I had left.

I went upstairs and took out a piece of paper.

Dear Alexi,

I began. This time I didn't think about what to say before I wrote. I just wrote.

Remember my friend Scott? The one I said was interesting? Well, he's also a lot of other things, like a jerk. And a girlfriend-stealer. Only, he just got out of the hospital, so I don't want to say anything bad about him. But he was going to leave Hector out of the bomb shelter, and I went along with it. We started working on it in case your country decides to push the button. (You know which button I'm talking about, right?)

But it turns out Scott was almost killed because our tunnel caved in on him. It was my fault. Not for doing the wrong thing in the building part, but for not stopping him from doing the wrong thing. It was my fault for keeping my mouth shut. I do that a lot. Shut up, that is. I even did that when my grandmother made me do this Russian twin thing. You want to know the truth? I didn't want a twin, but I didn't want to say anything in front of the rabbi because he'd think I was being selfish. I feel better about it now, though. At least I can pretend you're listening to me, even if you're not.

Do you like any girls in Russia? Have you ever done anything you're really sorry for? Do you have a plan in case of nuclear attack? Do you have any ideas on how to stop one? Because I still haven't come up with any.

Your twin (not really),
David

I went downstairs for my backpack. My grandmothers were in the living room. They were playing mah-jongg, but they might as well have been playing different games.

"What is this character?" said Wai Po.

"The joker," said Safta. "Haven't you ever seen a joker?"

"This is not mah-jongg," said Wai Po. "We do not play with jokers."

"Of course it's mah-jongg," said Safta.

"You see these characters?" Wai Po said, pointing to the tiles. "Does this say *a* or *b*? Does this say *king* or *ace*? No. There are Chinese characters, for a Chinese game. No jokers."

"This is not how you play," Safta said.

"No," said Wai Po. "This is not how *you* play."

My grandmothers looked up and saw me at the same time. "David," said Safta. "Come join us. I will show you how to play mah-jongg."

"And then I'll show you how to play *correctly*," said Wai Po.

"Homework," I said. "And I have to practice my Hebrew."

"You can practice in front of us," said Safta.

"I'm still not ready for an audience," I said. "And I have to mail my letter to Alexi."

"I'm glad you're becoming friends," Safta said.

"He hasn't even written back."

"Well, it takes a long time for mail to reach Russia," she said. "If it even reaches him at all. You never know. The government may take the letters."

"That's true," said Wai Po. "Or at least read them first."

Whoa. They were actually *agreeing* again.

"Why would they want my letters?" I said.

Safta looked at Wai Po, who did the answering. "Because it's something to take away," she said.

Around five o'clock, Scott's mom called and asked me to come over. "Scott's been asking for you," she said.

I wanted to make up an excuse, but then I remembered

that Rabbi Doug said visiting the sick was a mitzvah. Scott wasn't sick, but he was injured, which counted.

Scott was lying on the couch in his family room next to a snack table full of get-well cards. His right leg was in a cast, which I could see poking out of the bottom of a plaid blanket. He raised a hand when I walked in. "Hi."

"Hi." I stood in the middle of the room, not sure where to sit. I really didn't think I should sit on the couch because Scott was taking up most of it. I sat on the floor and wondered what we could talk about. I was pretty sure that the hole, Scott's parents, and our dubious friendship were off the list, which didn't leave a whole lot.

Scott had Olympic time trial stuff on TV. The announcer reminded us that the US had boycotted the last Summer Olympics in Moscow because the Soviets had invaded Afghanistan.

"How are you doing?"

Scott shrugged. "Okay, I guess." He tried to sit up a little and winced. "The doctor said I should stay home from school for a couple of days and take it easy."

"I can get you your homework," I offered. "If you want."

"I think my mom's worked it out with the school," said Scott.

"Oh."

We watched a guy shoot down a track on something called a luge. Instead of riding stomach down, this guy rode on his back.

"Luge is a pretty funny word," I offered. I said it, drawing out the soft *juh* sound at the end. Scott didn't laugh.

"I guess," he said.

"Did we ever have any trivia questions about the luge?" I asked.

"I don't know," said Scott. "I don't remember."

I picked at the carpet, wondering how much longer I had to stay.

"So, uh," Scott said. "Thanks for saving my life and all that. The paramedics said that if I'd been in there much longer, I would have gone into shock." My dad had given me a list of all the things that could have happened. Like brain damage due to lack of oxygen. Or inhaling some weird fumes if we dug deep enough. Loss of limb. Death. Somehow, it didn't seem right that death should be part of the list. It should be on another list by itself.

"You're welcome," I told Scott. We could have been strangers talking. "Hector should get some credit, too," I added.

"Hector." Finally, Scott had some emotion; he sounded like he was spitting. "He didn't do anything. He just kept asking me questions about rivers in Africa."

Last week, I would have let that comment slide by. But this time I couldn't. "Actually," I said, "Hector is the reason we even went out there. I wanted to show him the hole and if we hadn't then we never would have . . ."

"So now he's a hero?"

"I didn't say that," I said. "I just said he was the reason we were there."

"It wasn't his," Scott said. "We had a deal. Until you started blowing me off for Hector." He tried to make it sound like he was joking, but his voice was too hard.

"Well, you've been blowing me off for Kelli Ann," I said. I tried to sound like I was joking, too. But it still hurt.

"Yeah." Scott stared at the ceiling. "It's not like it's our choice, though. My mom and her mom, they're like a divorced moms club. They go to each other's houses. Eat pizza and drink wine. Lots of wine. Kelli Ann and I just get the pizza. We're like their junior members or something.

"That Saturday Hector invited us to the movies? Divorced Moms Club. I didn't really want to go to Hector's house, but even if I had, my mom's pretty prickly about this stuff." He took a short breath. "Hector, man, and his perfect little family. Who wants to be around that?"

"The Clellands aren't perfect," I said. I'd heard them fight last year when I was over there. Well, they were speaking Spanish, so I couldn't be a hundred percent sure, but tone was everything.

"They went to *Disney World*," said Scott. As if that defined perfect.

"So when did you and Kelli Ann . . ." I couldn't bring myself to say the words, and I didn't know the international sign for dating.

But Scott knew what I was trying to say. "Wait. You

thought Kelli Ann and I were together?" He shook his head. "I told you, man, no relationships. Not for me. They just . . . implode."

Any relief I felt was instantly obliterated by guilt. Scott was right: I had been blowing him off. But not for Hector. I was ignoring him because I was too mad to do anything else. But I wasn't ignoring him anymore. When you see someone trapped at the bottom of a pit, a pit that you helped make, it kind of changes your perspective. You figure out that the real reason your friend's been preparing for the end of the world is because his whole world's gotten shaken up in ways that don't have anything to do with US-Soviet relations. In spite of what he was saying about relationships, Scott had gone out of his way to connect with one person. Me. "I'm sorry," I said. "About your parents."

Scott buried his face into the couch cushions for a moment. "My ribs," he said. "They hurt."

"Do you want something?" I asked.

He shook his head.

"You'll get better, though," I said. "Right?" I realized it wasn't clear whether I meant getting over the broken ribs or the divorce.

"So they say." Scott's answer wasn't any clearer. "Meanwhile, I'm supposed to take it easy. It's torture, just lying here with nothing to do." He stared at the ceiling. "They fought over that, too. Whose *couch* I should lie on."

"My grandmothers fight a lot," I said.

"It's different when it's your parents. I'll trade you, any day of the week."

We watched more luging. Some of the guys looked as though they might shoot right over the side of the track, but really, after a while, they all kind of looked the same.

When I was younger, having fun was a lot easier. One time, Hector and I spent a whole afternoon playing paper football on Hector's dining room table. We said we were playing for the world championship. Hector finally scored with the ball just hanging off the table, seeming to defy gravity. We jumped up and down and yelled *did you see that?!* Because it seemed absolutely incredible and amazing and it didn't matter who won or lost. It was enough that we saw something incredible and amazing together.

Was that what growing up meant? Having less fun? If so, Rabbi Doug hadn't covered that in any of our little talks. Or maybe we were stuck between the little-kid fun age and the being-able-to-drive fun age.

"I'm pretty tired," said Scott.

"I'll see you later," I said. I tried not to look relieved to go.

"*Xinfeng*," said Wai Po, holding up an envelope.

"*Xinfeng*," I responded agreeably. Wai Pao had started trying to insert Chinese lessons when and where she could to even things out. Half the time I didn't know what she was saying but I tried to play along.

Chinese had rising and falling sounds, too, like Hebrew, though when I told Safta that, she said, "I can't hear it." And when Wai Po showed me that in the traditional Chinese books, the writing was read from right to left, I told her that Hebrew was read the same way. She just said *hmph*, which made me think that they were really more alike than anyone liked to think.

We were working on the rest of my bar mitzvah invitations, the ones for the in-town guests. Apparently, we were already late because people should have six whole weeks to think about whether they were going to come or not. Wai Po was doing most of the writing, because she could do calligraphy, and she would do it for free.

"*Qing ni ge wo shi ge xinfeng*," she said.

"Yes," I said. This was my standard answer for when I got lost in Chinese. I figured I had a fifty-fifty shot that way.

Lauren reached over and handed Wai Po some more envelopes. "Wai Po asked you to hand over ten envelopes, dummy," she said. She heard Wai Po, even though she had on her Walkman.

"Lauren," Mom said sternly. "Don't call David a dummy." I noted that she didn't say that I wasn't actually a dummy. Then, to me: "So we have the suit. We still need a tallis."

That's the prayer shawl I would wear for the ceremony.

"I've taken care of that already," Safta said.

"That too?" my mother said. "When?"

"A long time ago," Safta said. "A surprise. What else?"

"I think we're all set on the program," my mother said. "If there are no more changes, I'm going to send it to the printer."

I looked over at Lauren, who was bobbing her head as she stuck the invitations into the envelopes. She was being a good sport. She didn't have to help.

"Actually, I think I have an idea for the program," I said.

"Well, give it to me soon. And you haven't given us your friends list yet."

There was a reason for that, which was that nobody was on it besides the kids in my Hebrew school class. There were lots of acquaintances I could invite, but it was the people I should have been the most sure of that confused me. It didn't help that winter break had started, so we couldn't even talk at school. And I still hadn't decided whether or not to invite Kelli Ann.

"You should send one to Alexi," said Safta, who was in charge of stamp licking. "Seal's grandson sent one to his twin."

I wondered if my cousin Jacob would ever know how much extra work he had made for me.

"I just hope he doesn't get in trouble, for receiving the invitation," Safta said. Bao Bao padded into the room, but instead of sitting by Wai Po, he sat by Safta. She made a face at him.

"He won't receive it," said Wai Po, finishing an envelope with a flourish. She sounded certain.

"Maybe I shouldn't send it, then," I said.

Wai Po looked surprised. "Of course you should send," she said. "Just because he will not receive it does not mean you should not send."

That seemed like funny advice with the price of overseas stamps. But Safta agreed.

"What if Alexi emigrates to Israel? You could go to Israel and if you go you want to be able to tell Alexi that you sent an invitation."

Then she added, "Seal's grandson is going to Israel, you know."

I finally sent out all my bar mitzvah invitations, including one to Hector and one to Scott. I thought maybe that would be a start toward fixing things. I checked the mail three days in a row, but they didn't send back their response cards. Maybe they'd been confiscated, like Alexi's letters. There were still invitations left, so I decided to send one to Kelli Ann, too.

Which gave me an idea. In my Torah portion, Moses was in the desert, getting ready to receive the Ten Commandments, and he was doing pretty much everything by himself: teaching the Jewish people, listening to them, being the judge. Then his father-in-law showed up and said, "The thing is too heavy for you. You are not able to perform it alone." Maybe I needed help, too.

Kelli Ann could be part of the help I needed. And that meant that I needed to call her on the phone.

I got Kelli Ann's number from the phone book and then I spent forty-five minutes working up the courage to dial. Bao Bao followed me, along with a cloud of scary thoughts. *What should I say first? What should I say second? What if she didn't say anything?*

"Why do you keep walking around the house with the phone book?" asked Lauren. Her button for the day said, ASK ME HOW. So I did.

"I need to prepare for a phone call," I said. Being prepared, that's what was key: for nuclear war and for talking to girls.

"You're going to call Kelli Ann, aren't you? That girl from Thanksgiving?"

"No. Maybe. Yes." I pounded my head against the door frame. "Yes."

"Okay," said Lauren. "Don't be afraid and if you run out of things to talk about, ask questions."

"What kinds of questions? Trivia questions?"

Lauren shook her head. "You make this sound like rocket science." She got an index card and dictated some questions to me. *How is your break going so far? What did you do today? What did you get for Christmas?*

"How do you know these things?"

"Duh," said Lauren.

I looked down at the card and wrote another line. *Have you seen* The Right Stuff? I pretended that if she said no I would ask her to go with me even though I had already seen the movie on Christmas day, after we went out for Chinese. I also made a note to joke about the Hanukkah wreath, since that was the thing we had talked about the most.

Then it was time.

I grabbed the hallway phone and took it into my room. The cord was just long enough.

Ring.

What if I got the answering machine? Should I leave a message?

Ring.

If I left a message, would I say "This is David" or "This is David Horowitz," because there were three Davids in our grade? And a number, I should leave our number, right? And maybe say it twice, just to be considerate. Was there enough time for that? Why didn't I write down a leaving-a-message script?

Ring.

I was just going to have to wing it.

"Hello?"

I took a deep breath, and said, "Hello," back.

Kelli Ann was really good at talking on the phone. It made me wonder if she was used to talking to boys. I wasn't used to talking to girls on the phone (or anywhere else) except for Safta, on Sundays, when she still lived in New York. "So listen, I was hoping you'd do me a favor," I said.

"That depends on what it is," she said, which was probably smart.

Here was my plan: I wanted Kelli Ann to plant the idea that the trivia team really needed to get together and practice. A lot. Because we were *known* and failure was not an option.

"That sounds easy," she said. "I can do it tomorrow at Wine and Whine."

That was what she called it, instead of Divorced Moms Club.

"Good," I said. "Maybe it will keep them from talking about the fallout shelter."

"I don't think anything will stop them from talking about that," Kelli Ann said.

"Yeah, we really dug ourselves into a hole," I said. I hadn't meant to make a pun, but Kelli Ann laughed. It sounded like bells.

When we hung up, I realized that I never had to use my cheat sheet, not even once.

I called Hector's house next.

"David!" said Mrs. Clelland when she answered the phone. "Where have you been? Hector has been home all this time, mope, mope, mope. His father just dragged him out to the movies."

I wasn't sure what to say to that, so I said, "Would you tell him I called, please?" I was about to say good-bye, but then I realized that getting Mrs. Clelland on board was probably even better than talking to Hector. I gave her the details, and I said that Hector could spend the night, too.

"I am sure Hector will love that. I will tell him. How lucky Hector is to have a friend like you," she said.

I crossed my fingers, and hoped that what she said was true.

Kelli Ann called the day after Whine and Wine. I nearly

dropped the phone when Wai Po handed it to me.

"I just wanted to let you know," Kelli Ann said, "that Scott said he's ready to start practicing again. He practically wanted to start right then, but he had left Trivial Pursuit at his dad's house."

"How did you convince him?" I asked.

"I just said some things about the honor of our school. And how, if the team lost, everyone would blame him because he was captain."

Even if they weren't going together, she knew him better than I wanted her to; she knew how his brain worked.

"I also told my friends that this was a really big deal, and that you guys weren't practicing," she said. "So I think they'll put the pressure on. Now you owe me."

"I do?" I said. The idea of owing Kelli Ann anything was kind of dizzying.

"Yup."

"I can repay you by bringing honor to the school," I said. "If we win." *Or with a movie?* I thought. But I couldn't get that part out.

Hector was the first to arrive on New Year's Eve. He was frowning when I answered the door.

"My mom said I had to come," he said. "For practice." He wasn't carrying anything for a sleepover.

Part of me had hoped that Hector would just show up, and everything would automatically be okay again. But I was going to have to work harder than that. It's like Rabbi Doug was always saying about my Torah portion: It wasn't going to seep into my brain by osmosis; I needed to work.

It didn't get any better when Scott showed up with his mom.

"Call me, for any reason, okay?" she fretted. "I just don't know if this is too soon."

"I'm *fine*," said Scott, even though he was leaning on crutches.

Normally, Hector would have said something—he was good with older people, parents especially. This time he just stood there.

Mrs. Dursky brushed Scott's hair out of his eyes. "You boys won't roughhouse, will you? The doctor said no roughhousing."

Scott jerked his head away from his mom's hand. "We're playing *Trivial Pursuit*, Mom."

After she left, my mom put Scott's backpack in the living room instead of the basement so he wouldn't have to go up and down the stairs. Then it was just the three of us. Hostile (Hector), Irritated (Scott), and Nervous (Me). We were like the rejects of the Seven Dwarfs, the ones who didn't make the cut.

"Let's get this over with," said Hector. "I told my parents I'd call them as soon as I was done."

We set up the game board and started running through the questions. Hector was all business. He didn't even eat any of the snacks my mother had set out for us.

Hector landed on Science & Nature and got an easy question about the initials *FM*. This was for a pie piece.

"Freddie Mercury!" I shouted. Hector's favorite band was Queen. I hummed a little "Bohemian Rhapsody" and waited for everyone to laugh. They didn't.

"Frequency Modulation," said Hector. He reached into the bag and got his green pie piece. He sounded almost bored.

Was this the way it was going to be from now on? No more joking around?

At least Scott seemed to be feeling better. He got three pie pieces early on. And in typical Scott-know-it-all fashion, he supplemented his answers. After informing us that the "first hole" in golf is in St. Andrews, Scotland, he added,

"St. Andrews is the home to the Royal and Ancient Golf Club, you know."

"Got my application in right now," I said. Hector didn't say anything, though he did take a chocolate pudding pop when my mom brought some of those into the living room. She must have known what was up, in the way that moms know that sort of thing, because she usually has a no-chocolate rule where the living room was concerned.

Even though Scott was doing well, he kept getting impossibly hard Entertainment questions. "Why would any-one even know these?" he asked.

"It's called *Trivial* Pursuit," said Hector, "not *Real and Important Things* Pursuit."

He had a point. But sometimes it was nice to know a little about a lot of different things. Just last week, Safta made a comment about Tony Bennett, and I mentioned "Boulevard of Broken Dreams." I thought she was going to fall over.

Hector got two more pie pieces in a row, which meant he had them all. He made it to the center of the board, where Scott and I got to pick the category for the final question. We picked Sports & Leisure. Hector always got stumped by Sports & Leisure.

I didn't want the game to end. The end of the game would mean that Hector would go home, and that would be it.

Then Scott said, "You guys should spot me a piece."

"What?!" This was the most emotion Hector had shown all night. "Why?"

Scott spread his arms open. "Because I almost died."

Hector had been fiddling with the cards, flipping them back and forth in the box, but now he stopped. "Yeah, you almost died, you jerk. Because you built your stupid survival hole without me."

"It's called a fallout shelter," corrected Scott.

"You would have let me die."

"You should be thanking us," Scott said. "If you'd been building it with us *you* could have died. Without a nuclear war. You could have been the one in the hospital. Not including you was the nicest thing we ever did."

This was the clearing-the-air part, only the air still felt polluted. How was I supposed to apologize for what we did? For what we didn't do. *Sorry I made you eat Spam and lied to you and sorry that we were going let you die when the bomb hit. Want another pudding pop?*

"Come on, don't you think a sick person should get one measly pie piece?" Scott shifted on the couch. "And by one measly pie piece, I am referring to the pink one." Pink was Entertainment, the hardest one.

"No," said Hector. "I don't think so. Just give me my question."

Scott and I exchanged looks. Scott shrugged, as if to say, *give him what he wants.*

It was my turn to read the question. I read it slowly, to

make it last longer. "*What numbers on the first roll of the dice make you crap out?*"

Hector wrapped his hands around his head and stared at the ceiling. "I *know* this," he said. "My dad played craps in Vegas once. It's two."

"Two?" I said, trying to delay the end.

"Yes, two," said Hector. "Definitely."

"Is that your final answer? This is for the win." I used my game announcer voice.

"Yes, that's my final answer."

"Number two?"

"Yes!" shouted Hector impatiently. "NUMBER TWO MAKES YOU CRA—"

Hector never did finish his sentence. At least, I couldn't hear him. Scott and I, and then, finally, Hector, were laughing so hard that my mom came in from the kitchen to see what was going on. Scott said that laughing made his ribs hurt, but it seemed like the pain wasn't so bad as before.

"You guys reek, you know that?" said Hector.

"Maybe it's number two," I said, which set everyone off again.

And maybe that was how you forged peace: You wore the other side down until they couldn't be mad at you anymore. You made them realize they didn't hate you as much as they thought.

Or maybe you just waited for one really good poop joke.

We woke up early on New Year's morning, even though we'd stayed up late the night before. Hector had borrowed my pajamas, which were way too small on him, along with a toothbrush, which we let him keep.

Scott wanted us to go see the fallout shelter.

I wasn't sure that was a good idea, but Scott said he hadn't even been in his father's backyard since the night the tunnel had caved in.

So when my dad drove Scott to his dad's, who had New Year's custody since his mom got Scott for Christmas, Hector and I went along. While the dads talked about football, we went to the backyard and stood around the hole. Hector looked a little awkward, like he didn't know if he should be there or not. The hole was smaller than I remembered. You could still see the footprints from the firemen's boots.

It was a brand-new year: 1984. It was also 5744, according to the Jewish calendar, and in a few weeks, it would be

Year of the Rat, on the lunar calendar. Being Chinese-Jewish-American meant that there was always a fresh start coming somewhere; I had a feeling I might need them all.

"You know," said Scott, leaning over the hole, "if we put in some supports . . ."

"NO," Hector and I said at the same time.

"Okay, okay," said Scott. "I was just speculating."

"I want to know," said Hector. "Did you guys ever think about where you were going to take a dump in your fancy hole?"

Scott and I traded glances. That was a detail we had overlooked.

"So much for two heads being better than one," I said.

"Three would have been better," said Scott. "Though I still say not including you may have been the nicest thing we ever did for you."

"Just don't do it again," said Hector.

I looked back into the hole and wondered if we could have made it more than a day down there.

"We should fill it up," I said. "So some little kid doesn't fall in."

Scott still couldn't do much, so Hector and I kicked some of the dirt back in, careful to stay on flat, unbroken ground. After about twenty minutes, it still wasn't full, but it didn't seem quite as dangerous. The hole was officially closed.

"My dad will probably fill it in some more," said Scott. "He's going to put this place on the market."

"I thought he just bought it," I said.

"He wants to live closer to the city," said Scott.

"Does that mean you'll change schools?" asked Hector.

"No," said Scott. "My mom's not moving, just my dad. You guys are stuck with me."

"Darn," said Hector. "Because I was all ready to take over as captain."

"Next time we do a project like this, we'll do more . . ." I said. I looked at the hole and tried to find the right word. Preparation? Research? Planning? Then I looked up at Hector and I knew what I should say, because what we needed to do was more talking and less leaving others out. "Next time we'll do better," I said.

Hector looked at me and nodded, as though he had heard not just the words I said out loud, but the other words that were inside my head. And then I said those words, too. "I'm sorry."

Scott didn't say anything, but he nodded. And for Scott, that was saying a lot.

I didn't get much mail on my birthday because everybody was saving cards for my bar mitzvah. But I did get a letter from Alexi. I had pretty much given up on him so I was surprised when it came in the mail, with blocky handwriting. One stamp had a picture of ship on it, and another of a guy with a beard who looked like our assistant principal. I didn't even wait to go upstairs to open it.

It was a short letter and it didn't answer any of the questions I had asked him. He told me that Moscow was the capital (duh) and that it had many great buildings and the most beautiful subway in the world. I'd been on the subway in New York, which no one would ever call beautiful, and the one in DC, which was sleek and new, but not what I would call beautiful, either. I suppose the Russians tell their kids stuff like that all the time so they'll be proud of their country. He also told me they had the world's greatest hockey team and had won the gold in five different Olympics, so there was a lot of bragging about Russia but there wasn't much personal bragging about himself, which was a good thing.

He didn't say anything about Scott and he didn't offer me any ideas for ending the tensions between Russia and the United States, so maybe it was like Wai Po said, and he hadn't received my letters.

But he did say "thank you."

"My family tells me what you are doing for me," he said. "Someday we will meet and I will shake your hand." Alexi never used the words *bar mitzvah,* but I knew what he meant. I looked in the envelope again and saw something I had missed: a photograph, no more than three inches tall.

It was a black-and-white photo, but you could tell Alexi had light-colored hair. He was wearing a thick sweater that looked like it itched. It was not the kind of thing you would see a kid wearing around Eisenhower Junior High. He had serious eyes and didn't smile. We did not look like twins. We didn't even look like brothers. But I thought, even with the dorky sweater, he looked as if he could be my friend.

I put the letter in my desk for safekeeping. Then I got out a piece of paper so I could write back. I decided I wouldn't mention the US gold medal win over the USSR in men's hockey at the last Olympics. Not until we knew each other better anyway.

We all went to the trivia tournament: me, Lauren,

Mom, Dad, Safta, Wai Po, and Bao Bao. Bao Bao had squeezed through the front door when we were leaving the house and hopped into the station wagon. Wai Po didn't have the heart to put him back in the house. "He is tired of being lonely," she said.

"He's going to be alone in the car," pointed out Safta.

"He'll be *less* lonely," said Wai Po. He sat in the middle, near her, while Lauren and I climbed into the wayback.

Bao Bao—the answer to the question *Who is the world's most spoiled dog?*

The contest was at Robinson. On our way into the school, Bao Bao started barking. Wai Po turned around and looked at him instead of the stairs. She fell with a thud.

"Mom, are you okay?" My mother knelt down by Wai Po. Dad tried to give Wai Po a once-over, but she scowled and shook her head.

"Check on Bao Bao," she insisted. "I'm fine." Then to me, she said, "Go on in. And don't miss any questions on China."

"Or Israel," added Safta.

No pressure.

Our seats were up on the stage. From there, I spotted my family sitting together. I also saw Scott's parents, sitting apart. Mrs. Dursky was sitting with Hector's parents.

"This is it." Scott gave us the world's shortest pep talk as he stored his crutches under his seat. "Don't blow it."

Right away, the team from McLean showed that they were the team to beat. They got question after question correct. They even knew that James Madison was the shortest president.

We huddled together. "Would you have gotten that?" asked Scott.

Hector and I shook our heads. "Everyone knows Lincoln was the tallest, but no one talks about the shortest president," said Hector.

The McLean team missed the next question, which meant that they lost ten points. No one buzzed in with a guess. We were holding on to every point we'd earned.

The team from Chantilly got the next question.

Then the moderator asked: "*Whose basketball court in Washington, DC, is known as the highest court in the land?*"

The room was silent.

"Do you think they mean the Bullets?" whispered Hector.

"I've been to a Bullets game," I said. "The Capital Centre isn't particularly high, and besides, it's in Maryland."

"Thirty seconds," said the moderator.

"The highest court in the land is the Supreme Court," said Scott. "And it's in Washington, DC."

"Judges play basketball?" asked Hector.

"Let's find out," said Scott. "No risk, no reward." He raised his hand. "The Supreme Court."

"That is correct," said the moderator. "There is a basketball court on the fifth floor of the Supreme Court building."

Yes. We were on our way.

An hour into the game, we were smack in the middle of the pack, ahead of the teams from Falls Church and Arlington, but behind McLean and Chantilly.

We knew that the first woman in outer space was Russian cosmonaut Valentina Tereshkova, that 10 percent of the earth was covered with ice, and that Dolly Parton's middle name was Rebecca. We knew a bunch of sports questions, too, including the distance between first base and third base (127 feet) and that Sir Barton was the first horse to win the Triple Crown.

Slowly, we inched into second place. We needed one more question to tie, and two more to win.

I'd been feeling bad because Scott and Hector had answered the questions in the crucial moments of the game, to get us started and to edge ahead of Falls Church.

"*Complete with artwork, chandeliers, and marble walls,*" the moderator read, "*what Moscow institution also served as an air-raid station during World War II?*"

Scott leaned over and whispered: "Too bad your Commie pen pal isn't here." Even after his near-death experience, Scott was still Scott.

"The Kremlin," said the captain from Chantilly.

"Incorrect," said the moderator. "Anyone else?"

"That's what I would have guessed," whispered Scott. "The Commie bigwigs would protect themselves first."

"Wait," I whispered. My mind churned through the information I knew about Russia, information from books and information from letters, like the one I'd gotten from Alexi.

He said he took the Moscow Metro to school, *the most beautiful subway in the world.* If their metro was like ours, part of it would be underground.

"The Moscow Metro," I said. "Their subway. That's the answer."

Scott gave me a look. "Where'd you come up with that?"

"No one?" said the moderator.

"It's the Moscow Metro."

"I don't think they even have subways in Russia," Scott said.

"It's not like you know any better," I argued. Now I felt like I was playing for me and Alexi, for pride, for world peace. Maybe even for Kelli Ann, who had dance class and couldn't make it. "Say Moscow Metro. No risk, no reward, remember?"

"If you're wrong . . ." Scott said. But I knew what would happen if I was wrong: we'd be down another ten points. Down, and possibly out. He raised his voice. "Moscow Metro."

"That is correct."

I needed to ask Alexi more questions about his hometown. And to say "thank you."

In the end, McLean won by buzzing in on a couple of

easy questions before the moderator even finished speaking.
Was there any kid in America who *didn't* know that Pluto was
Mickey Mouse's dog? Still, I'd gotten a number of questions
right. I knew how many people were at the Last Supper, which
Scott said was weird since I was Jewish. I knew that all
the raisins in the United States came from California, that the
Chinese had invented the compass, and that Daniel Boone
was a member of the General Assembly of Virginia. I spoke
out and did my best. And second place was pretty good.

"Especially against the eighth graders," Lauren
pointed out.

"Good job," said Safta. "I only wish I could have heard
more of the questions."

"The acoustics were fine, Ma."

"No," said Safta. "I couldn't hear because of the
moaning." She pointed at Wai Po. "She's not fine."

Wai Po had her right hand hidden in her coat. "No, no. Everything is okay."

Dad walked over to her. "Don't be scared," he said gently. "Just let me see."

When Wai Po took her hand out of her coat, Mom gasped. My grandmother's hand was swollen to nearly twice its normal size. One of her fingers, the one with the ring from Wai Gong, looked blue, like the finger of a dead person.

"Let's stop by my office, shall we?" Dad said.

Since Dad worked at the hospital, they bent a lot of rules for us in the ER. Wai Po didn't have to wait for a room; they took her right away. They also let us stay back with her, even though there was a sign saying only one family member could stay with the patient. I wondered whether Scott's mom or dad sat with him when he went to the hospital.

Wai Po sat hunched over on the gurney. We let Mom take the only chair. She was looking greenish—she hates blood and other medical stuff. Safta stood in the middle of the room, crossing her arms. She didn't want to touch anything because of germs.

The doctor walked in and said hello to Dad. Her badge said Dr. Fisher. Then she examined Wai Po's finger for about a minute and said, "We have to get this ring off to relieve the pressure."

"You can't get it off," said Wai Po. "My finger is too swollen."

"We have a special device just for cutting the ring," explained the doctor. "We'll get it off in a jiffy. I promise."

"No." Wai Po pulled her hand back against her body. "You must do it another way."

"You could lose that finger if we don't remove the ring," said Dad. "It's cutting off the circulation. We could be looking at gangrene, and then . . ." He didn't say the rest, but we knew.

Mom made a sort of burping noise in her throat. "Lauren, why don't you take Mom to the waiting room," said Dad.

"I think I'm going to go sit in the car," said Safta.

"Fine, go," said Dad. That left Dad, Wai Po, Dr. Fisher, and me.

Dr. Fisher softened her voice. "There's nothing to worry about, Mrs. Lin. There's no risk of the ring cutter hurting you in any way. Do you want me to show it to you?" She sounded like she was talking to a little kid.

"No one is cutting this ring," said Wai Po. She tucked her chin low and I saw that she had tears in her eyes.

Dr. Fisher sighed. "We're running against the clock," she said to Dad.

"Give us a minute," said Dad. He ran his hand over his head. Then he motioned for me to step outside the curtain with him.

"Got any ideas?" he asked.

"Me?" Dad must be feeling really desperate, asking me

for ideas. Unfortunately, *How do you get your grandmother to change her mind?* was not a question that came up in Trivial Pursuit.

"I can't make your grandmother do anything against her will," he said. "But we can't let her lose her finger over that ring."

One of the nurses entered through a side door, letting in a gust of cold air. For that moment, we could hear a dog howling. Bao Bao.

Dad shook his head. "See if you can get him to stop. And if you think of anything, let me know. Soon."

When I walked out to the parking lot, I found Safta holding Bao Bao at the end of a makeshift leash. He had stopped howling. "First he wanted out of the car," said Safta. "And now he wants to go in the hospital." Bao Bao strained at the end of the leash, which Safta had made out of her purse strap. "Stop it, Boo Boo. You'll choke."

I told Safta that we hadn't made any progress with Wai Po. "Oh my," she said, twisting her own wedding ring. "I know what she's feeling. I haven't taken off my wedding ring since your grandfather passed."

"*You* should come talk to her," I said. "You actually know how she feels."

Safta shook her head slightly and looked away. "I wouldn't do any good."

"Sure you would," I said. "You have lots in common." When she didn't say anything, I added, "We're running out of time."

Safta sighed. "Who's going to watch the dog?"

That gave me another idea.

When Safta and I headed back into the hospital, Safta told me to put my shoulders back and walk with purpose. "No one will stop you if you look like you know what you're doing," she told me.

It was a wonder I wasn't already a spy, with Safta and Wai Po being so sneaky.

"No," Wai Po said when she saw us. She held up her good hand to hide her face. "Go away."

"But we brought you a special visitor," I said. I opened my coat.

"Bao Bao!" Wai Po's face lit up. Bao Bao leapt out of my arms and into her lap, and began licking her face. She stroked him. "*Xiao pangzi,*" she said. *Little fatso,* I translated in my head.

"Now," said Safta. "What's this I hear about you not letting them take care of you?"

Wai Po looked away. "This ring is very important to me. I cannot have it cut."

Safta held out her hand, showing Wai Po her wedding ring. "I know how you feel. I haven't taken this off since I lost my Joseph, may his name be for a blessing."

Wai Po nodded.

"But if I can take mine off, you can, too," said Safta. And just like that, she slipped off her ring and held it up. "Taking the ring off doesn't mean you love him any less."

Wai Po hesitated. "I was going to give this ring to Lauren," she said, her eyes filling up. "So she would not forget me."

Old people worry about some pretty strange things, I guess. I thought about the Thanksgiving dinner, the flying attack latke, the pinecone poops, and the world's most embarrassing trip to the mall. "Wai Po," I said, "and Safta. We have lots of memories. Even without the ring. We couldn't forget you even if we tried."

Wai Po actually smiled when I said that. And then Safta put her arm around Wai Po. "Did you know the sister of Mr. Pickens's son's wife is a jeweler? We'll have that ring fixed up and no one will even know it was cut. Good as new."

"And you'll still have a finger to put it on," I added.

Wai Po looked at my grandmother, and then at me. "Okay," she said.

It was like all the doctors and nurses had been waiting for Wai Po to change her mind. As soon as I told Dad, they descended, carrying a tiny diamond-blade saw that looked like a can opener.

"We'll just wait outside," Safta said. She shuffled toward

the curtain, holding her black wool coat tightly closed. We were nearly home free.

But as soon as the doctor approached Wai Po with the saw, Bao Bao sprang out of Safta's coat like one of those people jumping out of a birthday cake. Everyone turned and stared.

And Bao Bao? Bao Bao ran. He slipped under the curtain and disappeared.

Dad looked from me to Safta and back again. "What the . . . who brought . . ." He struggled to form a question.

From the other side of the curtain, we heard someone say, "Hi, doggie!"

"Do you want me to lose my job?" Dad said. "GET THAT DOG!"

The ER was a maze of hallways and tiny rooms. Even though there were counters and stretchers in our way, you could see where Bao Bao was by people's expressions and a few shrieks.

I was never going to catch him. And Dad was going to lose his job.

A woman in a surgical mask threw up her hands. "How'd that dog get in here?" I heard her ask.

We would have to cancel the bar mitzvah. I wasn't going to become a man. And I was never ever going to have any kind of chance with Kelli Ann Majors.

I heard Safta running behind me. Then she stopped. She unsnapped her purse and pulled out a bag of dog treats. "Bao

Bao," she called into the air, pronouncing his name correctly for once. "Treat!"

What?

Bao Bao suddenly appeared and sat down in front of Safta. His whole bottom wiggled. "Pick him up," said Safta. "Then we'll give him the treat."

I picked up Bao Bao, trying not to fall over from the thoughts spinning in my head. As we walked out of the ER, with Bao Bao happily munching on a hot dog treat—not his regular brand—I put it all together.

"You're the reason why Bao Bao has been getting so fat," I said. "You've been giving him snacks!"

Safta didn't say anything.

"Safta, you have *dog treats* in your purse, and you don't own a dog," I said.

Safta turned a deep shade of pink. "That dog," she said. "Always bothering me, sniffing, barking. I decided I would put a stop to that."

"By stuffing him with treats," I said.

Safta pulled back her shoulders. "I am making a friend from an enemy."

"So you like Bao Bao now?" I said, holding up the dog.

Safta reached out and carefully scratched Bao Bao behind the ears. "I've dealt with worse," she said.

My bar mitzvah was only a few days away, and Safta

was in full-on prep mode. The knishes, which were for a lunch at our house after the service, but before the Safta-inspired fancy reception, were all done and filling up the freezer.

"I still need to make the rugelach," said Safta, checking over her list.

I looked at Wai Po, who was sitting by herself in the living room, stroking Bao Bao with her good hand. Her other hand was still in a huge white bandage.

"What about the Chinese restaurant?" I asked.

Wai Po shook her head. "Too much money after the hospital," she said. "It doesn't matter anyway." She nodded toward Safta. "She is making enough food for an army."

But it did matter. Maybe if you'd told me a few weeks ago that I'd only have one kind of food at my bar mitzvah, I would have been happy. Now I knew, though. Real peace doesn't come just from not having conflict. It comes from everyone feeling right with the world.

I went upstairs and grabbed Lauren. Then we trooped back downstairs together. "Will you tell us how to make stuff for the reception?" I asked Wai Po.

She didn't even look at me. "What stuff?"

"Chinese stuff. We don't need to order it from the restaurant. We can make it."

Wai Po seemed to think about it. Then she said, "Too much work."

"No," I said. "Come on. You tell us what to buy and what to do, and we'll do it."

"Whatever it is," Lauren said. "We can make it."

Safta came out of the kitchen. "I can help, too."

"You don't have to," said Wai Po.

"We're *machetunim*," Safta said, as if that decided it.

"What does that mean?" I asked. My Yiddish was about as good as my Chinese.

"It means that she is the mother of my son's wife, so we're relatives," she said. "It means we're family."

Wai Po nodded.

We made *shumai*. And *char siu bao* with beef. Curry puffs. And eight-treasure rice. And then we stopped because Wai Po said that since she wasn't feeling well, she would "take it easy."

Shumai was a kind of dumpling, with a piece of carrot or a pea on the top. It looked fancy. "It should have pork," grumbled Wai Po as she directed us on how to make the filling. "But ground chicken will do." Safta was the best at making *shumai*. "You make a few thousand kreplach in your lifetime, and you know how to make a dumpling, no matter what you call it," she said.

"When my hand gets better, I will make *that*," declared Wai Po.

I wasn't sure whether to call it the Treaty of Shumai or the Kreplach Concord. Whichever it was, I had negotiated it. And the Trivia Treaty—I'd negotiated that one, too. I hadn't saved the world or forged peace between the Russians and the Americans, but I'd made peace in my own backyard. And maybe that was the place to start. I went upstairs and finally started to work on my paper for Mr. H.

"World Peace begins in your own backyard," I began. For once, it didn't sound like I was just writing a bunch of BS, the way I had for science. For once, I was pretty sure I was on the right track.

The morning of my bar mitzvah, Safta stopped by our

house early. My stomach already felt like it was full of Pop Rocks and seeing my grandmother made me think we were late for the synagogue. I didn't even have my socks on yet, and I had no idea where I'd put my tie.

"I have something for you." Safta handed me a flat box, about the size of a magazine. But when I opened it, I found a long, whitish piece of fabric with blue stripes and fringes on the end.

"A tallis?" I said.

"I told you I had taken care of it," my grandmother said.

I could tell it wasn't new, because it had a couple of yellowy age spots on it. I tugged on the fringe and wound it around one of my fingers. That's when I knew whose tallis it was.

"Grandpa's?" When he was alive and we visited for Rosh Hashanah, I would sit next to him in the synagogue and play with those fringes whenever I was bored and got tired of counting the colors of different yarmulkes.

Safta nodded. "He wore this for his bar mitzvah," she said. "He wanted you to wear it at yours." She wiped her eyes, and then she gave me the pouch that went with it, velvety blue, with some of the velvety part worn off.

Wai Po came outside and cleared her throat. I wondered if she was going to give me something, too. But instead, she opened her hand.

"They fixed my ring," she said.

I took the ring and examined it. The outside looked just as it had before, but the engraving inside had been altered, by a blow torch or something, when the jeweler welded the ring back together. Then I looked more closely.

"Look," Wai Po said. One of the letters in my grandfather's name—the name the engraver had misspelled—had been cut out. The other letters were closer together now, making a word. "It says *Shalom*. The Hebrew word for *peace*."

Safta and I stared at the ring. I didn't know that Wai Po even knew any Hebrew. "It's a sign," said Safta.

"Yes," said Wai Po.

"And you guys, you won't fight today, right?" I said. "Because the ring says we should keep the peace."

"David," said Safta. "We don't fight."

"Not at all," agreed Wai Po.

"That would be undignified," Safta added.

"The Chinese word for peace is *heping*," said Wai Po.

I kept my mouth shut. Sometimes you have to speak up for peace, but sometimes you just have to be quiet.

_____

I drove to the synagogue with my parents and Lauren in one car. Safta drove Wai Po in the other. I'd been worried that they would bring Bao Bao so he wouldn't be lonely again, but my mother talked Wai Po into leaving him home with the TV on for company.

At the synagogue, I said hello to a few people as they came in. Seal hadn't arrived yet, but lots of other people had, including my uncle Josh, who told me that during his bar mitzvah he had mispronounced a word and said "toilet" in Hebrew by mistake. Seeing all those people made my palms sweaty, so finally Rabbi Doug took me to his study until it was time for things to start. "The Green Room," he called it, even though his office was beige.

"I haven't had anyone pass out on me yet," he said.

"There's always a first time," I told him.

Rabbi Doug put his hand on my shoulder and looked me in the eye. "You're going to be fine. It's the waiting that's hard."

I went to the bathroom, once more, just to be sure, and reminded Rabbi Doug to use my middle name. Then it was time.

My father helped me drape my grandfather's tallis around my neck and showed me how to kiss the fringes. I hoped it would bring me luck and help me remember how to read the words.

"We are pleased for you to join us today as David Da-Wei Horowitz is called to Torah to become a bar mitzvah," Rabbi Doug said.

That sounded funny. Until then I'd thought of a bar mitzvah as a thing—not as a person. Not as me.

A mitzvah meant two things. It meant commandment, and that I was of the age to accept them. And it meant good deed. I hadn't done a lot of good deeds, but I was starting to. I hadn't saved the world, either. But maybe it wasn't all on me. Maybe I just had to start going in the right direction. And maybe if I did, other people would follow.

I led the prayers that I'd learned and they didn't feel as fumbly as they had on the rabbi's couch. My voice started soft, but by the time I got to the prayer when we opened the ark, it was stronger. Rabbi Doug carried the Torah through the synagogue. I followed him, and waved a little when Scott, Hector, and Kelli Ann tried to get my attention from the back row.

Then I followed the rabbi back to the *bimah*, and we opened the scroll.

I will not say that it was perfect, but it was good enough that I felt like I'd kept my end of the bargain. When I was up there, the words didn't feel like just nonsense anymore. They came together, and some of the English words I remembered flashed across my brain, too.

Rabbi Doug had made me read the translation before I ever read the Hebrew, and it all came back to me, about

Moses on Mt. Sinai, and the whole mountain smoking—not because of a nuclear war, but because the Jews were getting the Ten Commandments. I had to explain it in my bar mitzvah speech, which came next.

When you're reading a speech in front of a bunch of people, you become aware of everything. The way your voice sounds. A cough. You're also aware of the fact that you wrote most of your speech at the last minute, which is maybe why it sounds a little bit like the paper you just handed in to Mr. Hudson. You are also aware of the fact that you have, hardly ever in your life, put this many words together without messing them up.

My ears were red from the second I said the words "Today I am a man." This was not part of the paper for Mr. Hudson but it is the same start as almost every other bar mitzvah speech that has ever been written.

"For a long time I wasn't sure what that meant," I said. "But now I have a better idea. It doesn't mean solving every problem in the world. But it means you have to try."

Then I said some stuff about how the Ten Commandments were written to help us solve problems and keep the peace in our own communities and our own houses. I also listed commandments of my own.

Listen to what others are telling you and what they're not telling you.

Speak up. Especially for those who can't speak for themselves. Or when poison ivy is involved.

Respect your family—they got you to where you are, and you're not going anywhere without them.

Don't leave anyone out.

Support your friends and construction projects.

Be brave, especially when it's hard, because that's when it's the most important.

Think big, whether it's a fallout shelter or science fair project.

Apologize when you're wrong.

Work for world peace by making peace where you are.

No matter how bad it gets, never push the button.

I saw some people nodding when I got to the button part; that meant that they had seen *The Day After*, too.

"Today I am being bar mitzvahed for myself and also for Alexi Abramovich, a Soviet Jew who cannot have a bar mitzvah of his own," I said. "We have never met, but I know that he's thirteen, like me, and that he likes hockey. I don't skate"—people laughed at this part—"but maybe someday I will. Maybe someday I'll find out more about Alexi. Until then, I hope his country and our country can find a way to solve problems together."

Then I thanked a bunch of people and everyone pelted me with candy that my cousin Ashley carried around in a small basket like she was a flower girl.

It was almost over.

Then the rabbi called my parents and sister to join me on the *bimah*. My mother squeezed my hand. "Now we will say a blessing with the people who helped get David to this day." I looked out in the front row and saw my grandmothers. They had helped get me to this day, too. I signaled at them to come up. Safta caught my look and came up immediately. My mother smiled and made room. Wai Po must have seen my signal, too, but she sat where she was. *Come on*, I mouthed, and signaled again. My whole family had helped get me to this day. The Jewish side. And the Chinese side. Because I was Jewish and I was Chinese. I wasn't half of each; I was all of both. Finally, Wai Po stood up and joined us. Rabbi Doug nodded, and gave the blessing.

Then we got to the part in the program that I had added just before we took it to the printer.

"Now," said Rabbi Doug, "we'd like to invite David's sister, Lauren, to lead us in the singing of 'Adon Olam.'"

Lauren joined me on the *bimah* with a big grin on her face, and I moved the microphone away from me and put it in front of her.

"Adon Olam" is a song that usually everyone in a congregation sings together. But my sister's voice was so sweet and strong and perfect that most of the congregation just listened instead. I think that surprised her, because she wavered for a minute, but then she kept going, center stage, like she was Pat Benatar. Or Lauren Horowitz.

When she was done, I gave her a hug without anyone even forcing me to.

Nobody choked on anything at the lunch at our house, which was just for out-of-town relatives. Mom brought an older woman in a dark purple dress over for me to meet. She looked very familiar.

"David," she said. "This is your grandmother's sister, your great-aunt Seal."

From the way Safta always talked about Seal, I had expected a towering force of bar mitzvah themes and invitations, and maybe some fangs and claws. Instead, there was a tiny woman who smiled just like Safta.

"I've heard a lot about you," I said.

"Hmmph. I expect you have." Seal held up one of the *shumai*. "Now this is something I haven't seen at a bar mitzvah before. Chinese food. I think I'll tell my daughter about it when she gets back from her ski trip. Your cousin Missy's bat mitzvah is in a year and a half."

I was a little surprised that she would want something Chinese at Missy's bat mitzvah, since her family had already achieved perfection with Jacob. I didn't think it would be Jewish enough for her. I didn't think *I* was Jewish enough for her.

She must have known, from my expression, what I was thinking. "For the record, I did say you didn't look Jewish once. I also said you were a beautiful baby. And now you are a handsome young man. You could be a rabbi, a speech like that." She reached out and pinched my cheek, which didn't seem like something you should do to a young man, but I was new to the position and didn't know all the rules yet. I could tell from the pinch, though, that she thought my bar mitzvah had been *done right*, too.

I couldn't wait to tell Safta about my conversation with Seal, from the *shumai* to the rabbi comment. Maybe it could be the beginning of another conversation.

The reception was at the Sheraton in a room downstairs. We had a DJ instead of a band, and we served dessert instead of a full meal so that we could keep things, as my dad liked to say, "within a budget."

Still, the photographer took a picture of him standing next to the table with his pockets turned out like I'd totally bankrupted him. (The photographer said he did this at most events, especially weddings.)

During the hora, everyone in my family took a turn in the middle, even Wai Po. Then my dad and some of his uncles and my parents' cousins, who I guess are my cousins, too, put me in a chair and lifted me up and I didn't fall off. Scott held on to the chair, too, but he wasn't in the circle going around it, because of his crutches.

After the hora, the DJ slowed things down so we could all catch our breath. "True," the sort of slow song I imagined playing for Kelli Ann in the fallout shelter, came out of the speakers. Now was the time. I looked around for Kelli Ann but she was on the other side of the room. I started walking. The room must have been a mile wide. I wondered if my parents paid extra for that.

"Faster! Faster!" screamed my cousin Ashley. Maybe she just wanted the music to go a little faster, but it sounded like she was urging me on. I picked up the pace.

Kelli Ann was wearing a lacy peach dress and she had her hair loose and sort of curled under.

"Faster! Faster!" screamed Ashley.

I went through a quick checklist.

Breath? Check.

Closed fly? Check.

Words in the right order? Check.

"Want to dance?" I asked Kelli Ann. For a minute I worried that she would say no. But when I saw her smile, I knew I'd be okay.

"Sure," she said.

I reached for her hand.

"Hey, folks," the DJ said at the very moment the song went into super-romantic mode.

"We're going to change things around at the request of my new friend Ashley. Here's 'My Bologna,' by Weird Al Yankovic!" The first strains of accordion blared out of the speakers.

Oh no oh no oh no. My first dance with Kelli Ann was not going to be to a song about lunch meat.

But Kelli Ann smiled even bigger. "I like this song, too," she said. And my heart lifted.

"Thanks for coming to my party," I said when we were dancing.

"You're welcome," she said.

"I never thanked you for saving the trivia team," I said. "I know maybe it seemed dumb, but . . ."

Kelli Ann smiled. "The game might be about trivial things, but friendships aren't," she said.

Man, this girl was smart. And pretty. And nice. But I didn't tell her that, because there were some things you didn't say out loud until you were totally, 1,000 percent ready. The important thing was, I was actually talking to her. And she was talking back. And Safta was on the side of the dance floor taking a picture, so there would be photographic evidence if her thumb didn't get in the way.

I thought about all the things I had to look forward to, like spending more time with my friends in a world that had not yet blown up, and eating all those leftover knishes and *shumai*. I was even looking forward to reading *1984* in 1984. We'd gotten through the first three chapters, and they were pretty good. But between my bar mitzvah speech and my paper for Mr. Hudson, I realized that the future didn't just mean the possibility of war; it meant the possibility of peace, too.

And maybe, just maybe, saying more things out loud to a girl I really liked.

We were the last ones to leave the reception, of

course. Seal gave Safta a small nod of approval before she left. They still weren't speaking—maybe they'd forgotten how— but I like to think my speech helped them connect. Then Safta and Wai Po came over to us with their purses and coats.

"We're going out," announced Safta.

"Now?" said Mom. "Aren't you tired?"

"Marjorie wants to check out a new restaurant for Chinese New Year," said Wai Po. "I told her Saturday night is the best night for checking on restaurants. It will not take long. We can check very fast."

"I'm driving," said Safta, as if that was a good thing.

"You drive like a crazy person," Wai Po said.

"I drive like a New Yorker," Safta said, standing up straighter.

They walked out together, and about one minute later, we heard the sound of a car scraping its way over a curb.

"I think we might have been better off when they didn't like each other," said Dad.

Even though it was late when we got home, I stayed up another two hours to open my bar mitzvah presents. It took a long time because my mother said we had to write everything down so I could send the appropriate thank-you notes. There were a lot of checks, enough for me to get something nice—a new bike or an electric guitar maybe—and enough to help Alexi.

So even though I was practically crawling up the stairs when it was time for me to go to bed "for real, this time," my mother said, I pulled out a piece of paper and started a new letter.

Dear Alexi,

We officially had our bar mitzvah today, and I didn't mess it up. Actually, it went pretty well. So I just wanted to say congratulations. To both of us.

Your friend,
David

P.S. I'm enclosing a copy of my speech, which I wish you could have helped me write. And if someone from your government reads it first: good.

Epilogue/Thank-You Notes

Dear Kelli Ann,

Thank you for coming to my bar mitzvah. And thanks for the Hanukkah wreath. (Ha ha.) You show true talent!

See you at school.

David

P.S. Thanks again for helping with the trivia situation!

Dear Hector and Scott,

Since you guys gave me one present, you get one thank-you note. Thanks for coming to my bar mitzvah. Thank you for the survival guide and the new Trivial Pursuit game. I can't wait to play.

Sincerely,

David

P.S. Thanks for the Spam, too. I'm saving it for the next time you come over.

Dear Uncle Phil,

I'm sorry you were out of the country for my bar mitzvah, but thank you for the Sphinx piggy bank. Say hello to the pyramids for me.

Love,

David

Dear Mr. Haggerty,

Thank you for my own personal copy of *1984*. You're right: It is great to read *1984* in 1984. Also, it is great to have a copy that doesn't have a bunch of sentences already highlighted.

Sincerely,

David

Dear Mrs. Cohen,

Thanks for coming to my bar mitzvah. I hope you had as much fun as I did.

David

P.S. Sorry about the knish. My mother would like you to know that I know that a knish should not be used as a football. I hope your shirt is clean now.

Dear Mr. Pickens,

Thanks for coming to my bar mitzvah. I hope you had as much fun as I did. Thank you for the copy of *Peony* by Pearl S. Buck. Who knew that Jews have been living in China for centuries?

Sincerely,

David

P.S. I am happy that you got a new dog. I would be happy to help take care of him.

Dear Aunt Tracey and Uncle Josh,

Thanks for coming to my bar mitzvah. I hope you had as much fun as I did. I appreciate your generosity and so will Alexi.

Sincerely,

David

P.S. Uncle Josh, Sorry that Mrs. Cohen screamed in your ear and that the knish landed on your pants. My mom would like you to know that I know that a knish should not be used as a football. I hope your pants are clean now.

P.P.S. Aunt Tracey, I'm sorry that a knish landed on your new shoes. A knish should not be used as a football, though from the way you kicked it, maybe it could be a soccer ball? Just kidding.

Dear Aunt Seal,

Thank you for coming to my bar mitzvah. I appreciate your generosity and so will Alexi.

Sincerely,

David

P.S. I know my grandmother was glad to have you there, even if she didn't say anything.

Dear Mr. and Mrs. Rosman,

Thanks for coming to my bar mitzvah. I hope you had as much fun as I did. I appreciate your generosity and so will Alexi.

Sincerely,

David

P.S. My dad says that you'd better be saving, since you have four kids.

Dear Rabbi Doug,

Thank you for tutoring me for my bar mitzvah. I appreciated all of the tips, for my bar mitzvah and for life in general. If I ever dig another hole, you're invited.

Your student and fully fledged congregant,

Mr. David Da-Wei Horowitz

Authors' Note

The Day After aired on one of television's four channels on November 20, 1983, when we were both in high school. We watched the show. Everybody did. And we were haunted by it. But we'd been fearful even before that. Cold War tensions left the specter of a mushroom cloud over much of the 1980s. When *The Day After* aired, it put our fears into moving pictures with special effects. The impact was far reaching—to the point that many believe the movie influenced President Reagan to begin working to limit nuclear arms. So when we began working on this story together, we knew that *The Day After* needed to be in there.

When we talked to other people about our idea for this story, we could tell who had seen the movie at the same time we had, by the way their eyes widened. But every generation has had its own concerns. Children growing up in the 1950s had to practice "duck and cover" in school. Friends remembered being haunted by the Vietnam War. By the Cuban Missile Crisis. By September 11. By gun violence. Each

generation has had an overarching threat and a correspond-
ing fear. And each generation has had to learn not to be
controlled by those fears. It is our hope that, like David in
our story, we will all continue to look for solutions, to speak
out for what we think is right, and to reach out to those who
need help instead of pointing fingers and pushing buttons.

Peace,
Madelyn and Wendy

Acknowledgments

Thank-you notes for books (like those from bar mitzvahs) are endless. And what if we forget somebody? So many people helped make this book possible.

Thank you parents, husbands, brothers, and *mishpocha*. Thank you to our kids: Graham and Karina; Matthew, Jason, and Kate.

Thank you, Lisa Sandell, for your careful reading and enthusiasm. Thank you, Scholastic, for your support of writers—and readers.

Thank you, Tracey Adams and Susan Cohen, for your wise and joyful words.

Thank you, Sara Lewis Holmes, Elisa Rosman, Lucia and Camille Saperstein, Evelyn Khoo Schwartz, and Mia Sorongon, for reading this story and for your insights into blending cultures. Thank you to our writing group, for supporting us in much more than writing: Jackie, Marty, Liz, Anamaria, Ann, Anna, Marfé, Carla, Moira, and Laura. Thank you Virginia authors and illustrators; we are so lucky to be a part of this writing community. An extra shout-out to Cece, Tom, Mary, Meg, Anne Marie, Rachael, Cecilia, Jeff, SCBWI, One More Page Books, and Hooray for Books.

For anyone who was traumatized by *The Day After*, this story is for you.

About the Authors

Longtime friends and critique partners, Madelyn Rosenberg and Wendy Wan-Long Shang began writing together when they figured out just how much dumplings and kreplach had in common.

Sports: *What author held her school record for the flexed-arm hang?*

Madelyn is the author of the How to Behave books, the Nanny X books, and *The Schmutzy Family,* a finalist for the National Jewish Book Award for Illustrated Children's Books. She is also the co-author of *Dream Boy*, with Mary Crockett. Visit her online at www.madelynrosenberg.com.

Entertainment: *What author can sing the alphabet backward flawlessly?*

Wendy is the author of *The Great Wall of Lucy Wu*, which was awarded the Asian/Pacific American Award for Children's Literature, and *The Way Home Looks Now*, Virginia's pick for the National Book Festival Great Reads list. Her website is www.wendyshang.com.